I0685833

A HEART RECONSIDERED

PEACOCK HILL ROMANCE BOOK 6

ELIZABETH MADDREY

Copyright © 2019 by Elizabeth Maddrey

All rights reserved. No portion of this book may be reproduced, stored in a retrieval system, or transmitted in any form or by any means—electronic, mechanical, photocopy, recording, scanning, or other—except for brief quotations in critical reviews or articles, without the prior written permission of the publisher.

Scripture quoted by permission. Quotations designated (NIV) are from THE HOLY BIBLE: NEW INTERNATIONAL VERSION®. NIV®. Copyright © 1973, 1978, 1984 by Biblica. All rights reserved worldwide.

Cover design by Jennifer Zemanek of Seedlings Design Studio

Published in the United States of America by Elizabeth Maddrey. www.ElizabethMaddrey.com

Publisher's Note: This novel is a work of fiction. Names, characters, places, and incidents are either products of the author's imagination or used fictitiously. All characters are fictional, and any similarity to people living or dead is purely coincidental.

1

―――――

"That was some party."

Claire McIntyre turned, her mug of coffee steaming in the cool morning air. Of course it was Danny. He had on the shirt and pants from the tuxedo he'd worn to the Founder's Ball the night before, but the collar was open and the shirt untucked. His feet were bare. None of that should cause a little curl of interest to bloom in her belly. But it did.

She gave herself a mental shake and pushed a polite smile onto her lips. "I can't take the credit. We just provided the venue."

His eyebrows lifted. "And organized the details. I've seen you running around the last six weeks.

Claire took a sip from her mug and watched the mist around the base of the lion head fountain that spanned the back of Peacock Hill. He'd been watching her? When? "Yeah, well, that's what I do. I handle details."

"You're good at it." Danny tucked his hands in his pockets and turned to lean against the stone rail on the edge of the portico.

"Thanks." Now that he was facing her instead of standing beside her, Claire couldn't avoid making eye contact. She glanced down. "Aren't your feet freezing? You should go inside before you catch cold."

Danny laughed. "Okay, Mom." He pushed off the rail and took a step toward the door. "Who was that guy you were dancing with last night?"

She'd danced with a lot of different men at the ball. Once word got out she'd been the organizer on the venue side, she hadn't had much time to sit and rest her feet. Apparently, thank you dances were a thing. But she'd only danced with one person more than once—the one man who was there without a date. "Jamie Fisher. Vanessa's brother."

"Vanessa the florist?"

Claire nodded.

"Huh. Okay." He paused, hand on the doorknob, and waited until she met his gaze to speak. "It really was a nice event."

"I'm glad you and Casey had a good time. Did she stay the night, too?" She hadn't meant to ask that. Claire took another sip of coffee and tried to act casual.

"Not like you mean. You really think I'd do that? Here of all places?" Danny shook his head. "She stayed out in the tower. I was here. Upstairs on the third floor. Wow."

Heat washed over her face, but she refused to back down. "How would I know?"

"I thought you knew me. Guess I was wrong." He disappeared back inside.

Claire sighed, her shoulders sagging. "Yeah, well, so was I."

AT THE TAP on her office door Monday morning, Claire minimized the window on her computer screen. "Come in."

Deidre poked her head in and grinned. "That was some shindig Saturday night."

Claire laughed. "Swanky, right? But I've already had an email from the board chair and co-chair. They both let me know they'll be recommending us to the committee as a permanent venue."

"Really?" Deidre's eyes lit up and she stepped completely into the room. She high-fived Claire before settling in one of the chairs facing Claire's desk. "That's excellent. Is it always November? It's a good time for us—weddings are down and there aren't as many groups looking to stay."

"Yep. First Saturday of November. It's not a done deal, but their recommendation is going to help. A lot." Claire studied her sister. The woman was an inspiration. She'd put it all on the line several times—first when she took over their dad's handyman business and turned it into a regional success that had reality TV calling. And then, when the host of that show ended up elbowing her out and trying to steal all the profit, she'd sold and come down to Peacock Hill to start over. Only Deidre could have seen the ramshackle shell of a building and imagined what it could look like with a little—or a lot—of elbow grease. And then she'd made it happen. "I'm proud of you, you know that?"

Dee flushed a pretty pink. "Yeah, well, same goes. As far as I'm concerned, you do all the hard work."

"Nuh-uh. You know me. I can grout tile, but that's about where my handiness ends. You made Peacock Hill what it is. It's an amazing accomplishment."

"Well, you took it and ran with it. A gorgeous mansion doesn't do a whole lot of good if it can't support you. I might have restored the place, but you brought it back to life." Deidre cocked her head to the side. "What's going on?"

"What do you mean?"

"I mean you can be complimentary, but you don't usually

push it. If I didn't know better, I'd say you were buttering me up before leaving."

Claire froze.

"Now is when you laugh." Deidre paled. "Laugh, Claire, before it's not funny."

"Here's the thing."

"No." Deidre lurched to her feet, her pregnant belly making the action less graceful than she normally would have been. "There's no thing. Things are not allowed. I can't do this without you. I don't *want* to do this without you. So don't you even think about saying you're going to leave me."

Watching the tears drip down her sister's face, Claire's shoulders sagged. She'd known this would happen. It was hormones. Pregnancy hormones were something she was becoming intimately familiar with now that her sister was expecting. That didn't mean she was immune to the guilt they spurred. "But Dee . . ."

"Don't." Deidre held up one hand while she used the other to wipe her face. "I can't talk about this right now. I can't believe you'd even think about doing this to me. To us!"

Claire opened her mouth, and she drew in a breath to speak, letting it back out slowly when her sister stormed from the room and slammed the door home like a shot. "That went well."

She drummed her fingers on her desk before reopening her resume on the computer. There was no harm in having a resume. It didn't mean she was definitely going to leave. It provided options. Options were good things, weren't they?

She spent thirty minutes fiddling with the document before she pushed away from the desk with a groan. This was just one of the problems with family businesses. She'd never needed a resume before. Now, here she was in her late twenties with no clue how to make one people would put on the top of a pile. Oh, sure, the Internet was full of ideas and recommendations, but how was she supposed to know which ones were the right ones?

Vanessa.

The answer was so obvious! Claire grabbed her phone and considered. A text was her preference, but how long would it take Vanessa to get back to her? As far as Claire knew, her friend was planning to open her flower shop as usual. So. A call. She tapped the phone icon and waited as it rang.

"Hey, Claire."

"Hey. Do you have a second?"

"Sure. It's quiet this morning. What's up?"

"You come from a business-oriented family, right? Do you know anything about resumes?"

"A little, I guess. Why?"

"Because I'm working on one and I don't know if it's any good. Or what I'm missing. Or anything like that. There are people I could hire and get help, but I don't want to make that investment unless I have to."

"Send it to me and I'll look. Or—hey—I could pass it to my brother. He's the business king. He'd be able to give you better feedback than me."

Claire pressed her lips together. Jamie. She got a little quiver in her belly. She'd gone over her dances with him on Saturday night more than once when she'd had some free time—and when she was supposed to be focused on something else—since then. "Yeah. Sure. That'd be good. Thanks."

"No problem. Want me to just give you his email? Cut out the middle man?"

Did she? "You don't want to see it?"

"Honestly? You're better off with Jamie."

"All right." Claire opened the desk's middle drawer and retrieved a pad of sticky notes and a pen. "Go ahead."

Vanessa rattled off the email and Claire jotted it down.

"Got it?"

Claire read it back.

"That's it. And there's someone at the door—let me know how it goes."

With a chuckle, Claire ended the call. She stared at the email address for the space of several heartbeats before taking a deep breath and opening a new email message on the computer.

She'd send it off and get back to work. There was a group of five women coming next Tuesday for a writing retreat and she still had a few final details to see to before then.

If some small part of her hoped Jamie would use the phone number at the top of her resume to reach out personally, well, that couldn't be helped. The guy was gorgeous. And kind. And smart.

And not Danny.

That last one was important. Moving on from Danny was the top item on her to-do list before the end of the year.

2

"**D**anny Kent." He held the receiver for his desk phone to his ear as his cell chimed with another text. Frowning, he glanced at the display. Casey. Again. He switched his phone to do not disturb and listened as his client outlined the changes he wanted made to the architectural drawings Danny had delivered on Wednesday. Of course Mr. Robertson couldn't have gotten back to him yesterday, when he would've had an entire day to get started on the changes. Now, it looked like he'd be spending at least part of the weekend working. Yay. "Yes. Yes, sir, I've got it. I'll—yes, Tuesday at the latest. All right. Bye."

He set the receiver gently in the cradle because he wanted to slam it. He couldn't afford to alienate the Robertsons. Not that he ever tried to do that, but sometimes he was okay with dispensing a little tough love. It just wasn't a great idea when the clients were close, personal friends of the agency's owner.

"Kent."

Danny fought a wince and swiveled in his chair. His coworker was leaning in the opening of his cube with a grin that let Danny know something unpleasant was coming. "Sly."

"Problems on the Robertson job? Need a hand? I told Martin you weren't ready for something this big."

"No. No problems. Just the usual changes that come with a new project. You know." He gave a careless shrug and started to turn back to his desk.

Sly cleared his throat. "Send me the list of changes, and I'll go over the design specs. We can't afford to make mistakes with a client like this. Not only is he friends with Martin, he's well placed. Lots of potential for new business."

Danny bristled at the implication that these tweaks had been part of the original order and he'd missed them. He gritted his teeth. "I consider every client important and a potential source for new business."

"That's exactly right, Danny. Hey, Sly, you don't have enough work in your own office?" Martin propped an arm on the top of the cubicle wall. "Saw we had a little pow wow going on here, thought maybe I'd missed a memo."

"No, sir. Sly just stopped by to chat." Danny glanced at the man and lifted an eyebrow. The two of them were even on the management chart. Sly was ticked that Danny had been given the Robertson job—but his proposal had been stronger, and Sly was the only one who wouldn't admit it.

"Good, good. Esprit de corps and all that, but maybe we should get back to work?" Martin's smile was gentle, but if Sly didn't feel the sting, he was even more oblivious than Danny thought. "Danny, if I could see you in my office in about thirty?"

"Of course." Danny checked the time.

"Great." Martin knocked on the top of the cube and glanced at Sly. "Since you're up and around, Sly, how about you go over the Fredericks job with me for a few minutes. I'd love a status update."

"Sure. Of course." He shot a glare at Danny before turning toward his own cube. "We've hit a few snags . . ."

Danny fought a grin as he spun back to his computer. Why was Sly trying to butt in on the Robertson project if his own projects weren't going well? Just looking for prestige most likely. If the guy would focus on his own work and pay attention to detail, he could be an amazing architect. As it was? Well, there was an office pool on how long before he got the axe. Not that Danny participated. But man, it was tempting.

He glanced at his phone as the screen lit up. Casey. Danny fought to stifle a groan. He'd better call her back. No matter how much he didn't want to. Things with her seemed to be winding to a close. She was getting clingy. Demanding.

He tapped the icon to return her call.

"Why haven't you answered my calls or texted me back?"

"I'm at work?"

"Yeah, well, so am I. It's important."

Danny closed his eyes and prayed for patience. "Sorry. What's up?"

"What are we doing tomorrow?"

"What are we . . . seriously?"

Her exasperated sigh came across loud and clear. "It's our five-month anniversary. We're doing something special, right?"

"Case—"

"No. Nuh-uh. This is important to me."

"And keeping my job is important to me, which means I need to work."

"You haven't said anything about working this weekend all week. A head's up would've been nice."

"I literally just found out. I need to tweak the—"

"Robertson file, yeah. You can still spare some time on Saturday night for a nice dinner."

Danny rubbed his temples. Technically, she wasn't wrong, but after a day hunched over his computer, he wasn't super excited about sitting at a candlelit table in a suit and tie.

"What if we hung out at Peacock Hill? They're having a movie night."

"No way. They don't like me. Plus, you don't spend anniversaries with friends. You don't even want to celebrate, do you?"

"I didn't say that." Danny checked the time as Sly's voice grew louder. He didn't need any of this today. "I have to run. Martin needs to see me in his office. Why don't you make reservations and just text me the details, okay?"

"Fine." It didn't sound fine, but hopefully she'd get over it. "Love you."

"Uh huh. Gotta run." Danny ended the call, pushed back from his desk, and stood. After a moment's thought, he locked his computer and file cabinet. He'd never been paranoid before, but something was up with Sly. If he was making trouble, Danny wasn't going to make it easy.

~

"APPRECIATE THIS, MAN." Matt punched Danny's shoulder before reaching for the seatbelt and settling back as best as he was able in Danny's tiny commuter car. "I didn't think I'd finish the restoration job quite so soon, but the owner was excited to get it immediately, so I figured I'd combine one last test drive and delivery and start the weekend with an empty slate."

Danny nodded. "Keep the customer happy, right? It's a good theory—what were you going to do if I had plans with Casey or had already left?"

"Call Azure." Matt shrugged. "She knew it was a possibility. We don't get up to Charlottesville for date night very often. We could've turned it into something fun."

"Why didn't you just do that? Dates matter, even now that you're married." Didn't his friend know that? He was an attentive husband, from everything Danny had observed, but maybe he was clueless about something. "Am I going to be on Azure's list because I gave you a ride home?"

Matt laughed, shaking his head. "No, man. If she'd wanted to come, she would either have followed me up or we would've arranged something. She's in the middle of a big painting—some kind of commission that has the gallery owner friend of hers in Atlanta calling every few days looking for an update. Her plan is to spend the entire weekend at the easel and see if she can get it done."

"That's a lot of time. How big is this painting?"

"It's one of those massive canvasses you'd see on a TV show in a two-story room. Just usually they have a colored square splatted in the middle. Or random flecks and stripes. Seems like those are quicker to paint. This guy wants a landscape." Matt shrugged. "Also I get the feeling she isn't super happy with it. Working under pressure isn't her thing."

Danny nodded. He understood that. His afternoon chat in Martin's office hadn't been particularly bad, but it had been full of reminders that the Robertsons were personal friends and that Martin had put Danny on the project because of his ability. Don't let him down. Right. No pressure. "I'm working all weekend, too."

"I thought you handed in that big project on Wednesday? Didn't you say that was the plan?"

Huh. His friends did actually listen when he talked. He'd mentioned it on Sunday afternoon during lunch, but in that casual, "What's going on with you" kind of way where people nod and move on to someone or something else. "Yeah. The guy has some tweaks. Well, he called them that. They're actually pretty major when you're worried about the little details like making sure the roof doesn't collapse as soon as you get it on."

"Ugh. I hate that. Guy came in last week asking if I could lift his truck, and okay, yeah, I do that all the time. This guy, though? He wants it higher than is street legal. Gets ticked when I say no. Guess you can't just tell the client it can't be done?"

"I wish. But it *can* be done. It just changes the entire design. And I don't even mind that too much—I want the guy to be happy. I would even if he wasn't my boss' best friend—I just wish he'd figured out what he wanted before I sent him completed plans based on his prior desires. Who's to say I'll send him this and it'll be right? He could have another brainstorm in the middle of the night and I'll be, ha ha, back to the drawing board again." Danny gunned through a yellow light and onto the ramp for the highway.

"Sorry, man. I'll pray this is the end of the changes."

"Yeah. Thanks." Danny drummed his fingers on the steering wheel, frowning. After several seconds of silence, he glanced over at Matt. "Did you and Azure celebrate anniversaries when you were dating?"

"Anniversaries? Like what? Two months together? That kind of thing?"

Danny nodded.

Matt snorted. "No. Who keeps track of that once you're out of high school?"

"Casey, apparently."

Matt winced. "Ah. Sorry. I didn't mean—"

"No, I agree with you. She's supremely annoyed that I have to work this weekend. We're going out tomorrow night because it's our anniversary. She told me which, but I honestly didn't pay attention, and I suspect I need to figure it out before the inevitable quiz at the table of some fancy restaurant. Which means, of course, that I'll be hauling my tail back into Charlottesville, or, knowing Casey, maybe even Richmond, so I can spend too much on food that's marginally better than average. And I have to wear a tie." Danny felt the scowl working its way over his face. "Women are a pain."

Matt rubbed his neck. His voice was tentative. "Not all of them."

"That's fair. You and Jeremiah managed to find sane ones. Maybe Duncan, too, although Anna's . . . intense."

Matt chuckled.

"I don't know. Sometimes I wonder if it's worth it. I mean, really, I'm pushing thirty. I'm doing okay on my own. Maybe I don't need a wife and a family. All my friends are going to end up with kids, so I can be fun Uncle Danny and give 'em back when they're tired and cranky." He shrugged. "Maybe that's not such a bad life."

"I thought things with Casey were going well."

"I don't know. It's like we're on different wavelengths. Like this anniversary thing. If she'd had to work the weekend, I would've said, 'cool, no problem, next week.' Maybe I would've offered to drop dinner by so she had something to eat. But I sure wouldn't have pouted and made it clear that anything other than capitulation was going to be a big fight."

"It's obviously important to her."

"Why, though? I don't get it. We're not married. We haven't even been together all that long. Like what, four, five months? I could *maybe* see celebrating six months. But she did the same thing after one month."

"Should you have expected this one then? Be real, man, if the girl you're with is celebrating every four weeks, you need to pick up on it. Get a clue."

"I thought the ball last week could count. She said something about it being a great way to celebrate. Now she's saying 'love you' when she hangs up, so I try to avoid calling her. She doesn't put it on a text. What am I supposed to do with that?"

"You don't love her?"

"I don't *know*. I don't think about it. We haven't been together six months—it's a little fast to think we're in love."

Matt snickered. "You might need a new friend group."

Danny sighed. "Yeah, yeah. You're right. All y'all fell in love fast. And got married faster. That doesn't mean it has to work that way for everyone. Wouldn't I know if that's where things with Casey were headed? Shouldn't I know?"

"Not if you're not thinking about it. Praying about it." Matt shot Danny a pointed look.

Praying. Right. Next up was the conversation about coming to church more regularly. Was there any way to head that off at the pass? "I guess I'll do more of that. You and Azure talking kids yet?"

Matt jerked back, his head shaking. "We've only been married two months."

Danny fought a grin as Matt started listing the reasons they weren't even considering babies in the near future. He let his thoughts drift, tuning in just enough to nod in the empty places —that was a skill he'd honed dating Casey. Boy could she talk. Was she really in love with him? She'd never come out and said all three words as a short, declarative sentence. What did that mean?

Did being in a long-term relationship mean you had to second-guess everything your partner said? He'd thought— hoped—it would be the opposite. Why couldn't dating Casey be as easy as being friends with Claire?

Or at least as easy as that used to be. Claire . . . something was up with her. And she was either picking a fight with him or shutting him out, which meant he wasn't likely to find out any time soon.

Women were confusing.

3

Claire flipped down the visor and slid open the vanity mirror to check her lipstick. She had on about twice her usual makeup. Did it look like she was trying too hard? Deidre had whistled—but that was probably more older-sister teasing than anything. Whatever. There was no law against mascara. Or eyeliner.

She pressed a hand to her flip-flopping belly and drew in a deep breath. She was meeting a friend's brother for dinner. He probably just wanted to talk about her resume. He could've sent an email, but maybe Jamie was a hands-on guy. Or he was doing Vanessa a favor, so he figured he should do it all the way.

Just get out of the car, Claire.

She pushed open the door, grabbed the purse she'd borrowed from Anna, and slid out. She glanced around the parking lot. Was he here already? She had no idea what kind of car he drove, so there was no way she'd be able to tell.

After a steadying breath, she picked her way across the parking lot in the heels she'd talked herself into wearing. They really were the worst, most annoying shoes in the universe. But they made her legs look good.

Not that she wanted Jamie to notice her legs.

Probably.

"Can I help you?"

Great. It was a snooty restaurant. At least she was dressed appropriately. "Yes. I'm meeting Jamie Fisher."

The woman's eyebrows lifted and she offered a smirk that was probably meant to be a smile. "Right this way."

Claire wound through the tables behind the hostess, searching the dimly lit tables for Jamie. She spotted him a moment before they arrived at the table. He was on his phone, but glanced up as they approached and grinned.

Jamie scooted his chair back and stood. "Hi, Claire. I got here early and was catching up on some email. I'm glad you could make this work."

"Hi." Claire glanced at the hostess. "Thank you."

"Of course. Enjoy your dinner."

Claire chuckled.

"What's funny?" Jamie waited as Claire sat, then resumed his own seat. "She doesn't think I should be eating with you."

Jamie frowned. "Why would you say that? I don't know her."

"Woman thing. Don't worry about it." Claire opened the menu but didn't look at it. "I appreciate you taking a look at my resume. I didn't expect you to make a trip to discuss it in person."

"Well, I'll admit that wasn't my only motivation." He studied her a moment. "I enjoyed our time at the ball and wanted to get to know you better. Maybe I misread the situation, but I thought you might also be interested in that."

Claire blinked. Had he misread things? She'd enjoyed their dances. He'd been a little pool of calm in a night that was a swirling morass of anxiety. He was certainly easy to look at. Her face heated. "I would be. I guess it's been such a long time since someone was interested, I don't know how to pick up the signals.

And that right there is me in all my cringey glory. We can stick to the resume."

He laughed and reached across the table to lightly brush his fingers over her hand. "Don't be embarrassed. I stick my foot in my mouth constantly. So maybe we can tackle the resume first and then see what happens next?"

"Sounds good." She let out a breath and glanced down at the menu. The prices were high, which probably meant the portions would be tiny. She could always make a sandwich when she got home if she was still hungry.

A server appeared at the table and rattled off the specials. "Do you need a few more minutes?"

Jamie angled his head, his gaze locked with hers. "Claire?"

"I'm ready—" She could be, at least. If Jamie had been sitting here a while, he was probably anxious to eat. Claire glanced down at the menu again and tapped the listing. "I'd like the filet, please, medium rare, with the asparagus."

The server nodded and took her menu before shifting his attention to Jamie.

"I'll take the swordfish special, exactly as you described it. And could I get another soda? Claire, did you want something more than water?"

"No, thanks. I'm set."

"Very good. Enjoy." The server drifted away.

Claire tried to tug her gaze from Jamie's, but it was magnetic. And it was going to be awkward if they spent too much more time staring at each other. She cleared her throat. "So."

"Right. First, can I say you have an impressive resume?"

She barely managed to choke back a snort. "I really need you to be honest with me. If I leave Peacock Hill, it's going to upset my entire family, so it has to be worth it. I can't just pop off for some random job."

"I am being honest. You've done a lot for someone who's only twenty-six."

"You say that like I'm a child. How old are you?"

"Almost ten years older. So take my word for it, okay? I have a lot of life and work experience." He grinned to soften the words that would otherwise have made her bristle. At least he didn't sound condescending. Still, that was a bigger age gap than she'd realized. "Is that a problem?"

Could he read her mind? "I don't know. I don't think so. I figured you were maybe thirty. Thirty-two, tops. I'll be twenty-seven in March."

He chuckled.

Good grief. Could she be a bigger idiot? Her face was on fire—it was probably so red other patrons didn't need their candles to see. "You couldn't possibly care. Can we pretend the server just left and go back to then? I'll say thank you and then ask for your thoughts on how I can improve my appeal to prospective employers."

"I'll send you an email with a marked-up copy. I didn't have a ton of suggestions, just a few little tweaks. You have a solid resume, good experience . . . in fact, I was going to ask if I could send it down to our HR. We have three openings I think you'd be a good fit for."

Claire blinked. Three openings? At his company? "I don't—it's not because I'm friends with Vanessa, right?"

"I promise you, I don't do friendship or pity hires. Our company can't afford to carry a lot of dead weight. But when I see someone qualified—and I happen to know the person is driven, reliable, and capable? I'm going to try and hire them rather than letting someone else snap them up. If the fact that I'd also be interested in exploring a personal relationship with you makes that awkward, we can talk about it. I don't see a conflict of interest—none of the positions would report directly to me—so as far as I'm concerned, there's no problem with us hiring you."

What was she supposed to think? She snatched at the thoughts that swirled around, but they moved too fast. Nothing solidified. Throat dry, she reached for her water and took a long drink. "Thank you."

Jamie chuckled again. "Should I include the job postings with the marked-up resume?"

"Yes, please." That, at least, would give her something to look at. Maybe then she'd be able to put together a cohesive thought or two. Her stomach was knotted. It made no sense. This was exactly the kind of thing she was hoping for. So why wasn't she leaping for joy? "Are they all in DC?"

"Arlington, yeah. They're at headquarters." He angled his head to the side and studied her. "Is that a problem?"

"No. Of course not. I understand that leaving Peacock Hill means relocating." Claire ignored the little clutch in her heart. This was the right thing to do. It was time to be on her own—not employed by her family in one way or another. And having a job she could leave behind when she went home for the day? There were no words to describe how enticing that was. "My parents are up near DC still. It'd be nice to be able to see them more often."

"Great. Once you've had some time to look them over, let me know which ones—if any—sound like they'd be a fit and we'll set up some interviews."

"I thought you were going to send it through HR?"

Jamie shrugged, a little boy grin teasing the edges of his lips. "Being the boss has to have an advantage every now and then, doesn't it?"

Claire laughed. She shouldn't let him do it that way. Part of the point behind leaving, or at least thinking about leaving, was to be firmly out there on her own feet. Doing what she wanted.

Not taking handouts from her family. Still, he'd said set up interviews. That wasn't a guarantee. It was just a chance. She'd have to be an idiot not to take a chance when it was offered. This was one of those God things everyone talked about but she'd never experienced. At least it seemed like it. "I guess it does. Thanks."

"Ah, here's the food."

The server reappeared with their entrees. Once the plates were in place and he'd been assured everything was satisfactory, he disappeared almost as quickly as he arrived.

Jamie slid his hand, palm up, across the table. "Can I say grace?"

Claire nodded and rested her fingers in his. His hand was warm and smooth. There were no zips of electrical current running between them, but she supposed she couldn't believe everything she read in her secret stash of romance novels. It was exciting and new—maybe that's what the authors were trying to convey—because she definitely felt that.

He gave her fingers a light squeeze before withdrawing his hand and shaking out his napkin and spreading it in his lap. "Can you tell me why you want to move on from Peacock Hill?"

"Probably not coherently, if I'm honest. It just feels like it's time. And, I know it's an unpopular thing for people my age, but I'm tired of working for myself. I don't mind responsibility. It's not that. I just want a job that ends. Something that isn't constantly lingering in the back of my mind because if I stop for the night, or the weekend, then I don't have enough money for groceries." Which was a little more dramatic than the actual situation, but it didn't *feel* more dramatic. Sometimes, the pressure to be sure there were upcoming bookings woke her up in a cold sweat.

Deidre would tell her not to let it get that way. But how was she supposed to stop? Her entire family—well, other than her parents—was depending on her for their livelihoods. And now

Dee and Jeremiah were having a baby. How was she supposed to be responsible for a whole new generation, complete with college in eighteen years? It was too much!

Jamie just nodded.

Claire looked down at her filet and sighed. She cut off a tiny bite and popped it into her mouth. When she'd swallowed, she glanced at him. "Was that the wrong answer?"

"What? No. There wasn't a right or wrong answer. I was curious."

"You didn't say anything."

"I was listening. And trying to compare it to my own experiences. I didn't love being an entrepreneur either. At the time, I wasn't ready to go work for my dad. I think in a lot of ways it was because he was still very involved. So it truly would have been working *for* my dad. Not with him. Not just at his company. I thought I needed to prove myself." He offered a small smile. "I didn't do so well at that, but I learned a lot about who I am that makes me a better boss. And even still, I'm glad I wasn't the one who had to start the company from the ground up. Taking over for Dad? I can do that. So I understand what you're saying—at least a little."

Claire swallowed the lump in her throat. "You might be the first person who does."

4

Danny searched the sanctuary for the Peacock Hill gang. His friends always ended up sitting together—the space they took up on the row growing as new people were added to the crew. Everyone was married, of course. Even the contractors who did events at the place were falling like flies. First the wedding planner, and then the florist.

He fought a snicker.

The florist. No one had expected that woman to end up with the baker. The guy—Topher—seemed normal enough. From what he'd gathered, the woman had taken some getting used to.

Where was Claire?

Not that he cared for her sake. He just needed to tease her about her fancy date last night. Imagine his surprise when he'd pulled into the parking lot of a swanky restaurant and spotted Claire's car. At least he'd been smart enough to keep it to himself. Casey had picked up on enough conversation to know that the gang imagined him and Claire together. To say she was unhappy about that was a huge understatement.

It wasn't like he gave Claire any encouragement. They were friends. Period. He wasn't even sure they were that anymore.

The whole "how can you do this to Claire" bit that the guys tossed at him was all a big misunderstanding.

He had no feelings for Claire, and she had none for him.

Danny finally spotted the group and made his way to their pew. He tapped Claire's shoulder. "Have a good dinner last night?"

Claire turned and looked at him, puzzled. "What? Why?"

"Saw you. Looked fancy. Hot date?" He waggled his eyebrows and ignored the tiny niggle in his heart at the idea of her dating the slick, older guy she'd been with. He hadn't gotten a good look—no point in staring and making Casey ask what was going on. If it'd been anyone other than Claire, he could've asked Casey to look and see if she had any idea who Claire was with.

Pink flared on Claire's cheeks. "No. Just dinner with a friend. I didn't see you there. Big night with Casey?"

Danny shrugged. No point in getting into the idea of celebrating ridiculous anniversaries with Claire. She'd probably agree it was dumb, but everyone else would chime in and it would decline into Casey bashing. He didn't need that. "She wanted something nice."

Claire's smile was full of pity. "Stinks to have to drive all that way just for dinner."

"Yeah, well. That's what happens when your girlfriend lives in the city. It's not so bad. You must agree, you did it yourself. Anyway, who was the guy?"

"A friend, like I said." She angled her head to the side. "You didn't say hi, so why do you care now?"

He didn't have an answer, but another shrug probably wasn't a great idea. "Just commenting."

"Whatever." She said it mostly under her breath, but he still caught it.

Danny frowned. Yeah, they absolutely weren't still friends.

What had happened? How much did he actually care? "Can I sit with everyone, or is that not a good idea?"

Claire made a broad sweeping gesture with her arm and shook her head as she scooted down to make more room.

"So. What was that?" Matt nudged Azure down the pew closer to Claire and patted the space next to him. "You don't usually come to church itching for a fight."

"I wasn't trying—you know what? I don't think I can stay. I have a lot of work I should be doing. This was obviously a bad idea."

"Don't be like that, man. Take a joke." Matt stepped out into the aisle and grabbed Danny's arm. "Dude."

Danny shook him off. "Let it be. You're right, I'm in a bad mood. And . . . maybe it's time I took a break from all this. The commute. The gang. Everything. Casey's been pushing for more. Maybe I ought to give it to her."

"More. What does that mean? Don't walk off."

Danny shook his head and forced himself not to turn back. He lifted his hand—it could be a goodbye. It could be a "here's what you can talk to." Up to Matt. Right now, he had work waiting for him at home and some decisions to make.

"Danny Kent. You're headed the wrong way."

He stopped, fighting a wince, as Matt's aunt, Mrs. Patterson, planted herself in his path. "Good morning, ma'am."

"Where are you going, young man? The service is about to start."

"I'm not feeling well. I need to head home." It wasn't completely a lie. His stomach was twisting in uneasy knots. It was likely due to his friends turning on him, but he couldn't rule out germs.

Her lips puckered like she'd smelled garbage overdue for the curb, but she didn't say anything else. She just patted him on the shoulder.

Danny hurried down the steps to his car. Was it time to move on? Move out and to the city. The commute to Charlottesville every day wasn't exactly a dream. On the flip side, did he really want to live there? He was a small town guy at heart. The little house he'd been able to afford down here probably cost less than he'd have to pay for an apartment.

He could move in with Casey. She'd made the offer a month ago, and his rejection of that idea had been immediate. They weren't sleeping together—though she'd made it clear she wanted that, too. It wasn't as if he'd never gone there. He'd been to college and gotten caught up. And the guilt from those years of his life still dragged at him when he was least expecting it.

Casey said it was because he was too entrenched in the small town church life.

Maybe he was.

The question became: did he want to change that?

DANNY SURFACED from his computer enough to realize the pounding he heard was not just his head. Squeezing his eyes shut, he pushed away from his desk. Time for a break anyway. The changes for the Robertson project were finished, but there were always little tweaks to find. Things that might make it even nicer and, if he was lucky, make this the final version.

The pounding continued.

Danny strode toward the front door, stretching his arms as he went. He yanked the door open and, seeing Matt, scowled. "What do you want?"

"Good to see you, too, man. Can I come in?"

"Why?" Danny leaned against the door and studied his oldest friend. Well, one of them. Jeremiah wasn't here—probably too busy with his wife now that they had a baby on the way.

"Can't a guy just want to hang out with his pal?"

"Not one who's also a newlywed, no."

Matt simply lifted an eyebrow.

With a sigh, Danny stepped back and tugged the door open wider. "Fine. Whatever. Come in."

"Always so gracious. It's one of the reasons we're friends." Matt set a grocery store bag down on the foyer floor and pushed the door closed before pinning Danny with his gaze. "We *are* friends. Right, Danny?"

"Yeah, I guess. So?" Danny crossed his arms. Matt needed to hurry up and get to the point. There were decisions Danny needed to make—he'd been pushing them off all afternoon with the Robertson project as his excuse. With that out of the way, he couldn't put it off any longer.

"So why don't we sit down, pop open the chips and guac I brought, and you can tell me what's going on with you."

"There's nothing going on, and I'm not hungry." Of course his stomach took that moment to let out a growl that rivaled a feral cat.

Matt laughed. "Uh huh. Come on. It's chips and guac, man, you're not seriously going to tell me it's not your favorite."

For good or ill, Matt knew him. Danny's lips quirked. "Yeah, okay. You want a plate?"

"For chips?" Matt shook his head. "Please."

"Just thought being married might have civilized you some." Danny led the way to the living room and flopped into one of the two leather recliners that faced an enormous flat screen. He leaned forward and pushed a stack of gaming magazines and cereal bowls toward the center of the coffee table.

"You're gonna get ants." Matt opened the bag and pulled out the food.

"Thanks, Mom."

"Well, you are." Matt shrugged and popped off the top of the guacamole container. "But if you don't care, I don't care."

"I clean up every couple of days. I've been busy with work." Danny dunked a chip into the chunky green spread. "I can move them now if it bothers you that much."

"Nah. Sorry. Azure's a neat freak—that's rubbing off."

Danny nodded. Matt's wife, Azure, had been living in a teensy camping trailer for years before they got married. She probably had to be focused on neatness when her entire living space was less than half the size of his living room. "How's she doing living in a house?"

Matt snorted. "Fine. You'd think she'd never had less space. I guess it's true what they say, you fill the area you have. But we're never going to have clutter, I can tell you that."

"That's not a bad thing."

"Nope." Matt took another chip. "What's going on, man? Storming out of church isn't like you. You haven't been this touchy since you went off to college."

Danny's hand froze on the way to the guacamole. Matt knew about the girls in college. He and Jeremiah both did. They were best friends and, the reality was, Danny had needed their help when he made the decision to stop sleeping around. "That's not what's going on."

"Isn't it?"

"I won't lie and say Casey doesn't want that to be the case. But we haven't." He left off the "yet" that echoed in his mind. Hadn't he been working on a justification for exactly that most of the afternoon? The idea had played quietly in the back of his mind while he fiddled with the house plans. "And I'm not convinced it's that big of a deal if it changes."

"Dude."

"What?" Danny frowned and stabbed his chip into the

avocado. "You going to give me the spiel about how sex is something special designed to help solidify marriage?"

"Well, it is."

Danny shrugged. "I already blew that, remember? So what does it matter? If I ever get married, that glue's already gone."

Matt frowned.

"See? No response. 'Cause I'm right." Danny stabbed his chip in and out of the guacamole. "I thought you and Jer were on my case about following in your footsteps and settling down. So why are you all grumpy about it now?"

"Are you going to marry Casey? I didn't realize it was that serious. You're in love with her?"

"No, man, why . . . Look, she's a great girl. She says she loves me. Maybe, I don't know, maybe that's enough. It's better than being single."

"She loves you. But I didn't hear anything about you in there. Don't go back to being the guy you were in college. You didn't even like yourself when you were living that way."

Danny pushed the food away and leaned back, frowning. He wanted to deny it. Loudly. The problem was, Matt was right. He hadn't liked who he became in college. And as good as it felt in the moment to crawl into bed with someone, the next morning was another story completely. It didn't take much to remember just how sick to his stomach he got when reality crashed down. Usually with a hangover included. He sighed. "So, what? Only you and Jeremiah get to have wives and families? I screwed up in college so I don't get to have a life now?"

"Did I say that?"

"Kinda sounded like it, yeah."

"Well, that's not what I intended at all. I just want you to be careful. Remember when you came home the summer between your junior and senior years? How determined you were to get your life back on track with Jesus and how He wants us to live?"

"Yeah."

"What happened?"

Ouch. Danny pinched the bridge of his nose. What had changed? He could, if he tried, get back to the feeling of that fire in his spirit. "I guess I got busy."

Matt nodded. "It's easy to do. We've let our accountability group slide, too. Maybe we should start it back up."

"Why? It's not like either you or Jeremiah have any problems. And I sure don't need two babysitters."

"Oh, man, I'm sorry."

"What? Why?"

"Because if you think that? I've let you down even more than I thought. I don't want to babysit you. Neither does Jeremiah. And we both still have plenty of problems. Marriage isn't a magic pill. What are you doing Friday night?"

"Seriously? Friday night?"

"Right. Date night. Sorry. Saturday morning?"

Danny bit the inside of his cheek. It was an olive branch. The truth was, he missed his friends. If this was the way to reconnect with them, he'd take it. "Sure. Breakfast at the diner?"

"That'll work. Garage opens at 7:30—can we say six?"

Danny winced. "Seriously? Yeah, all right."

"Sweet." Matt reached into the bag of chips and withdrew a handful. He nodded toward the bookshelf of videogames under the flat screen. "Got anything new in there?"

"Why? You need your butt kicked?"

Matt laughed. "Me? No. But I'm pretty sure you do. Load something up."

"Why not? It's your funeral." Danny dusted off his hands and considered. It had been a while since he'd played something multiplayer. His gaze landed on a boat racing game and he fought back a laugh. That was perfect. Matt might be the king of cars, but when it came to steering in a game, the guy was worse than useless. He loaded up the game and handed Matt a controller. "Prepare to be annihilated."

"You wish."

"I know." Danny pressed the button to start the game and settled back into his chair. Something in his chest loosened. He'd missed this. Not just the idea of playing games with someone, but Matt in particular.

Casey would be annoyed when she found out.

His stomach clenched. Was any woman worth this much stress?

Casey was.

Of course she was.

Wasn't she?

5

Claire handed the women their keys and smiled. "If you have any questions, my number's on the back of the keychain. You can call or text—I'm usually around and will get back to you right away."

"You said we could use the main floor kitchen?" The first woman squinted at the key before glancing up at Claire.

"Yep. We just ask that you clean up after yourselves. There's a dishwasher you can load rinsed dishes into—don't worry about running it. I check on that periodically. And if something is labeled, please don't eat or drink it." Was there anything she needed to move out of the fridge? There shouldn't be, but she'd buzz down and check after making sure the ladies were set. "Beyond that, just enjoy your time."

"If trying to cram ten or twelve thousand words into a document each day can be enjoyable." The second woman rolled her eyes with a laugh. "I know we're supposed to love the whole process of writing—that's what we do, right? But I'll let you in on a poorly kept secret. Writing is hard. And most of the time? I hate every single word I put down."

"Until you get to the end, read it over, and decide it's not as bad as you thought." The first woman chuckled. "That's your process. Your artistic temperament. I'm much more even keeled."

"Oh yeah. Sure you are." Her friend snorted. "Thanks. Claire, right?"

"Right." Claire took a step back, easing away. "Feel free to wander the grounds and gardens if you need a break. There's a wedding on Saturday, but otherwise you five are our only guests."

"Would it be okay if we set up outside or in one of the rooms on the main floor when we need a change of scene?"

"Of course." Claire backed up, watching as the women unlocked their rooms. She waited a moment, but there were no exclamations, so hopefully that meant everything was satisfactory. She hurried down the stairs, pausing as she always did to admire the panoramic stained glass window on the main landing. What must it be like to be so creative? Well, creativity might not be her strong suit, but she could organize with the best of them. Better than many people could. And if being an artist meant crippling self doubt? She'd just go ahead and take a pass.

The retro-styled kitchen never failed to make her smile. Claire checked in the fridge, pulling out a six-pack of fancy flavored mineral water that her sister had stashed in there. She'd take it down to Deidre's apartment. With the cans tucked under her arm, she checked the cabinets. There were cracker boxes left by previous groups and a half-full box of cookies. The writers were welcome to any of that. If they didn't get eaten, Claire was going to have to chuck it all out soon anyway. She didn't want to be responsible for someone getting a stomachache from eating food that was stale.

Pushing through the swinging door, Claire nearly smacked into Azure.

"There you are." Azure frowned at the cans under Claire's arm. "Thirsty?"

"Ha. No. We have a group of ladies here through Saturday for a writing retreat. I told them they were welcome to whatever was in the kitchen—or they can use it to prep meals if they don't want to go into town, whatever. Figured I should take out anything they shouldn't use. Dee drinks this like it's going out of style, so I thought I'd move it down into her apartment."

"Never heard of seltzer as a pregnancy craving, but I guess it takes all kinds." Azure shrugged and fell into step beside Claire as she made her way to the basement stairs. "So. What was up with you and Danny on Sunday?"

Claire glanced over at Azure and fought a sigh. She'd really hoped that, having made it to Tuesday with no commentary, people would let it be. "Nothing big. I guess he saw me on Saturday when I went into Charlottesville to meet Jamie for dinner and wanted to tease me about it."

"Jamie? Vanessa the flower lady's brother? That Jamie?"

"He's the only one I know. I guess, technically, his name is James, but I don't think anyone other than his mother calls him that. Maybe his father, too." Please let that be the end of things. Claire tapped on Deidre's apartment door before fishing in her pocket for keys.

"Fancy dinner with Jamie?" Azure wiggled her eyebrows. "He's a good looking guy."

"Aren't you married?"

"Married. Not dead."

Claire turned and leaned against the wall beside the door. "I've never understood that. I mean, I get that maybe you can't stop a subconscious acknowledgment that oh, hey, that guy's attractive. But shouldn't it then be something you try to stop thinking about? Are you lining people up and deciding if Matt's better looking? What if he ends up not winning?"

"Whoa." Azure held up her hands. "I'm not constructing fantasies around the guy. He struck me as good looking in our two seconds together when we were introduced. I suppose I should have focused on his intellect or kindness, but given that the sum total of our conversation was an exchange of names, it didn't come into play. I apologize for thinking your boyfriend is attractive. From now on, I'll remind myself he's a troll."

"That's not—he's not my boyfriend. And you're missing the point." Claire shook her head and unlocked the apartment door. She poked her head inside and called out, "Dee? Jeremiah? Anyone home?"

When there was no answer, Claire pushed the door open and strode through the small entry toward the kitchen. She took a sticky note from the pad by the cork board hanging on the wall and scribbled a note. After affixing the note to the drinks, she tucked them in the fridge and left, checking that the door was locked.

Azure was still waiting in the hall. "So if he's not your boyfriend, why the fancy dinner?"

"I never said it was fancy."

"Okay, that's true. But Danny saw you there, which means he was on his anniversary date with Casey, and I'm willing to bet she wasn't up for a typical sit-down chain restaurant."

Claire closed her eyes. This was another big check mark in the "move out and away" column. There were entirely too many people in her business here. Sure, they were friends and they meant well, but honestly, why couldn't they leave it alone? "Right. You win. We ate at a fancy place. It wasn't a date. Or it mostly wasn't a date."

Azure's face fell. "You don't have to tell me. I'm sorry. I guess I thought we were better friends than that."

"Don't do that. The guilt thing. Just don't."

"It's not a guilt trip, I promise. I was curious about what

happened between you and Danny, and you answered it. He teased you about your dinner. You didn't appreciate it. Got it." Azure checked the time and tucked her hands in the pockets of her baggy, hand-painted overalls. "I should run. I'm sure the garage is fine, but technically I'm supposed to be there to grab the phone if it rings. Catch you later."

Claire watched as Azure disappeared into the stairwell. Great. Just perfect. She wanted to put the blame firmly on Danny's shoulders. If he hadn't been so obnoxious—storming out of church just because she'd had dinner with someone— none of this would be an issue. It wasn't as if Danny had ever asked her out. Not once, despite any number of hints she'd given that she was interested. He had to know she was halfway in love with him. Didn't he?

Of course he did.

No man could be that clueless.

"THANKS FOR FILLING IN, CLAIRE." Matt handed her a stack of Bibles. "Put one on every third seat or so. Most kids have the app, but I like to get them in a paper copy now and then, too, see if they remember what order the books are in."

Claire laughed. "I'm not sure I do. I'm so used to tapping on a list."

"Exactly." Matt pointed at her before dropping his attention to a stack of index cards. "Are you upset with Azure?"

"No." Claire moved between the rows of chairs and the assorted sofas and cushions that filled the youth area, dropping a Bible here and there for the kids to share. Should she call them kids? Probably not. Youths? That just reminded her of an old movie—a courtroom comedy her parents always watched when it came on. Whatever. Of course, choosing a word was better than possibly catching Matt's eye and having to talk about the thing yesterday with Azure.

"Okay. If you're sure."

"I'm sure. And if she has an issue, she should come talk to me, not sic her husband on me. Should I go home?" Claire crossed her arms and glared at Matt.

"No. Look, we're all curious. Dee told Jeremiah that you're threatening to leave. Danny's being a jerk and storming out of church. Now you're sneaking off to fancy dates . . . you've gotta know we're curious, but you don't say anything. What's the deal?"

"There's no deal. And there are so many words in what you just said that I disagree with. I'm not threatening. I didn't sneak. Danny, for all he's an idiot, didn't storm." Claire stifled the shriek that hovered in her throat. "And if I am considering changing jobs, don't you think all this—this hovering—might be part of the reason why? Danny's never going to ask me out. I think we can all agree on that at this point, so there's no reason for me to keep burning a torch. I have to move on. I don't know how to do that if I'm here where I run into or have to hear about him and Casey every time I turn around. Why can't anyone get that?"

Matt blew out a breath. "We do. I promise you, we get it. But none of us want to lose you—either of you. And now it feels like we're probably going to lose you both. Danny's talking about moving to Charlottesville."

Claire furrowed her brow. "But he has a house here. Why would he do that? Where would he live? Even if he can sell the house here—and that's not going to happen fast, it's not like we have a growing community. He's not going to get enough out of it to buy in the city. See? That's another reason I should go. Danny shouldn't feel like he has to give up the place he's lived his entire life just to avoid me."

"I don't think—" Matt broke off as the voices of a group of

teens echoed down the hall. "Can we finish this conversation later?"

"If you want." Claire placed the last Bible on a chair and fixed a smile on her face. She had no intention of resuming their talk. She wasn't going to be responsible for forcing Danny out of his home. She had to stay through Saturday—it was true that Deidre could easily handle the writers, but it didn't feel right to stick her with them with no notice.

So she'd stay until those ladies checked out on Saturday. And then there was the wedding. She should probably hang through that, as well, just in case. Deidre didn't love being involved with events like that. Of course, if—when—Claire left, Dee was going to have to figure out how to deal. Or she could hire another event manager. Could they afford that? Not that it was Claire's problem . . . but it was still something to consider.

Danny strolled in as the room was filling with teens.

Claire glanced at Matt and quirked an eyebrow.

Matt shrugged.

Okay. So Matt didn't know Danny was coming tonight either. That was something. It still smelled like a setup, but Matt wouldn't lie about something like that. It was one of the things she liked about him—he was honest to a fault. Which didn't mean someone hadn't set it up. Azure could be sneaky when she wanted to.

"Hey." Danny's hands were in his pockets as he scanned the room. "Good crowd tonight."

Claire could be casual, too. "Yep. I think some might be the new series Matt's doing. There's good, relevant discussion. The whole 'Christian worldview' thing sounded dry and intimidating, but Matt does a good job keeping it practical."

"Beats studying Jonah for the billionth time."

Claire glanced over at Danny, but he was still watching the room. Was Jonah a random pick, or had he also heard that she was considering leaving Peacock Hill? Even if she did go, she wasn't being Jonah. She wasn't running away. If anything, she was running to new opportunities—looking for where God wanted to use her next.

Maybe she hadn't been praying about the decision quite as much as she should, but she could fix that. Besides, if job possibilities were dropping into her lap didn't that mean God was blessing the idea of her move?

"Jonah's not so bad. There's a lot to learn from his story. But practical application is good, too." Claire shrugged and changed the subject. "Have you made plans for Thanksgiving yet?"

"My parents are heading out to my brother's place near Chicago. I could go, but I don't really want to travel on the busiest days of the year. Plus, they're driving, so I'd either have to take the whole week off to go with them—and maybe get them to cut their trip short—or I have to try and fly. I looked at prices, and I think it's too last minute at this point. Are you guys having a big to-do at the Hill?"

"Of course. You should come. There's always plenty and it beats a microwave dinner."

Danny chuckled. "How'd you know? I'll double-check but go ahead and put me on the list, would you?"

"Sure. Just you?" That was casual, right? But she had to ask. It'd be awful if he showed up with Casey and they hadn't set a place for her. It'd be awful if he showed up with Casey. Period. She *had* to figure out a way to get over him. Even if it meant leaving.

Danny nodded. "Just me. Casey's heading up to her folks' place in Maine."

"Why aren't you going along?" What was she doing? Why did she ask that? "Sorry. You don't have to answer. I'm just surprised."

"It's a fair question. I—"

"All right, gang, let's get started." Matt clapped his hands for attention and the teens settled, their conversations dropping to whispers before stopping completely. "Great. Danny, you want to open us in prayer?"

Claire bowed her head. She didn't hear the prayer. She was too busy making up reasons Danny and Casey weren't spending Thanksgiving together and wondering if that meant there was still even a sliver of hope that he'd notice her.

"Six a.m. should not exist on Saturday mornings." Danny slid into a booth at the diner and scowled at the empty mug. "Where's the coffee?"

Matt grinned. "It's coming. She's putting on a fresh pot. I'm glad you could make it."

Danny grunted.

"I'm not late." Jeremiah jogged to the table and plopped down next to Matt. "Morning."

"Mr. Grumpy over there isn't quite awake yet." Matt chuckled and pushed his mug toward the edge of the table as the waitress approached with a full coffee pot. "Thanks, Myra."

"Course, hon. Y'all know what you want yet?"

Danny slid his mug over and scrubbed a hand over his face. "You still have the chocolate chip pancakes?"

"For you we do. Full stack?"

"Please." Danny grabbed his mug and glugged down half of it. He pushed it back toward Myra with a sheepish smile. "Maybe some bacon with it?"

She nodded and topped off his coffee before glancing at Matt and Jeremiah.

"Are the chocolate chips only for Danny, or can other guys get in on that?" Jeremiah dumped four creamers into his coffee and stirred.

Myra chuckled. "Bacon, too?"

Jeremiah nodded.

"And you, hon?"

Matt shrugged. "Why not make it three for three?"

"Easy enough. Give me a holler if you need something else." She turned, aiming for the lone man seated at the counter.

"How come none of you ever told me Claire had a crush on me?"

"Seriously?" Matt shifted to look at Jeremiah. "You want to field this one?"

"Nope. It's too early and I haven't had my coffee yet." Jeremiah took a sip from his mug. "How did you not pick up on it? And also? I'm pretty sure we did and you were all 'we're just friends.'"

"First up, I don't sound like that." Danny tapped on his mug. "Second? I didn't think you were serious."

"How is that our fault?" Matt shook his head. "We told you. You ignored it. Why is this coming up now?"

"I might have gotten to youth group earlier than expected on Wednesday." Danny shrugged. "You and Claire sounded like you were having a serious conversation, and I didn't want to interrupt."

"So you eavesdropped instead?" Jeremiah shook his head. "Not cool, man."

"I was going to leave. Then I heard my name. What was I supposed to do?"

"Not eavesdrop." Matt grabbed a napkin from the dispenser and wiped up the coffee that had dripped down the side of his mug. "You really didn't know about Claire?"

"We were friends. Are friends? Were. No, I didn't even

suspect. Why wouldn't she say something?" Wasn't it the twenty-first century? Surely a woman could make the first move if the guy she liked wasn't picking up on clues. Or, okay, it could be a scary proposition to do that, but still. It wasn't right that he'd gone two years without it being clear.

Myra brought out their food and topped off their coffee again.

Jeremiah poured syrup over the top of his pancakes. "Would you have done anything differently if she had?"

"What? Of course I would have." Danny spread butter over his top pancake then carefully maneuvered it to the bottom of the stack so he could repeat the process with the three other pancakes.

"What?" Matt crunched into a piece of bacon.

"What what?" Danny frowned and cut out a triangle of pancake from the stack.

"What would you have done differently?"

He would've asked her out. Obviously. It was obvious, wasn't it? Or would he have ignored it in order to maintain their friendship? "There's no way to know, is there? I didn't know so I can't Monday morning quarterback it. It's not like I can go back in time and find out."

"Fair point." Jeremiah pointed his pancake-laden fork at Danny, syrup dripping into a puddle on the table. "So what are you going to do now that you do know?"

"What's to do? I'm with Casey. Things are serious. Ish. I missed my shot."

Matt frowned. "What's 'seriousish'?"

"You know, man. We talked about this."

"You're still thinking of moving up there? Moving in with her?" Matt reached for his coffee. "I thought we got past that."

"I don't know. She's really pushing. At some point don't you have to just give up on being old-fashioned and realize that we live in the world we live in? I mean really, it's cool that you two managed to save sex for marriage. But how realistic is that for everyone? It's like saying everyone can be, I don't know, Iron Man. The odds are astronomical."

"Uh huh. That's a great rationalization, Dan, it really is. Except for one thing."

"Yeah? What's that?"

"We don't get to pick and choose the parts of the Bible we follow. And it sounds to me like you're working really hard to excuse a choice the Holy Spirit is trying to steer you away from." Matt glanced at Jeremiah. "Anything you want to add?"

"Nope. I think you hit it all. Unless it's worth bringing up the time I drove to your dorm to sit with you all night because you were worried you were going to hurt yourself."

Danny turned to look out the window. He tried to forget those days. The days when depression had clung to him like a fog that just wouldn't dissipate. He was better now. "That was a long time ago."

"Sure. But you remember why you ended up there, don't you?"

"Jessica." Danny closed his eyes. The pain that sliced across his heart was almost as bad as when it had been fresh.

"You loved her. You thought she loved you."

Danny swallowed. "And then she had an abortion. Just 'Oh, by the way, I was pregnant but I took care of it.' Why are we talking about this?"

Matt leaned forward. "Because, Danny, you're flirting with the possibility of doing this all over again."

"Casey takes the pill." Danny shook his head. "I know, I know, that's not the point. Except it's part of it, isn't it? She won't get pregnant, so there won't be any need to go down that road."

"Because birth control never fails, right?" Matt punched Jeremiah's shoulder.

Jeremiah snorted. "Oh yeah, for sure. We planned to get pregnant right away. That's exactly how that happened."

Danny poked his fork in and out of his pancakes, making neat rows of punctures across the surface. "So what? What do I do? Casey isn't going to stick around forever if our relationship doesn't progress."

"So maybe she's not the one for you. Honestly, if you were one of the kids in youth, I'd be telling you to run in the other direction. She's pressuring you when she knows it goes against your belief system."

Danny waggled a hand from side to side.

"What's that mean? She doesn't know that?" Matt frowned. "How can she not know that?"

"We haven't really talked about it. I mean, I've mentioned church. She doesn't say anything bad . . . I don't get the feeling it matters to her one way or another." Danny set his fork down. "And yes, saying it aloud I realize how it sounds." He let out a resigned sigh. "I have to break up with her, don't I?"

Danny looked up and saw his two best friends nodding. Great. Just perfect. But a tiny flicker of something light stirred along the edges of the dread that settled in his gut.

Maybe breaking up with Casey wouldn't be so horrible.

He pictured her reaction and winced. Okay, it was going to be awful. But he couldn't shake the sense that it was the right thing to do.

"How'd it go?"

Danny tucked his phone in his pocket and glanced at the rapidly emptying sanctuary. He'd snuck in the back—late—to try and avoid this, but he'd missed his chance to scoot out before everything was over. Still, it was like Matt had been looking for him. Maybe he had. Danny shrugged. "How was it supposed to go? It was awful."

Matt gave Danny's shoulder a sympathetic pat. "But?"

"Yeah, yeah. It feels right. I can't say good, because I don't think you're supposed to feel good when you dump someone, but I can go with right." And, if he was honest with himself, it didn't hurt like he'd expected it to. There were even twinges of relief. "She keeps texting me, though."

"Why?"

"I guess she figures I'm going to change my mind if she pesters me enough? I don't know. I didn't think I left her any doubt about the fact that we were done."

"Why don't you come up and have lunch with everyone? We're grilling. You know Jeremiah makes mean skewers."

Danny's mouth watered. Matt was right—everyone praised Jeremiah's nachos, but the reality was, his kabobs were even better. That might have something to do with Danny's preference for chunks of steak and chicken over tortilla chips. Either way, it wasn't an opportunity to miss. "You sure?"

"Why would you ask that?" Matt scowled at Danny.

Danny hunched his shoulders. "I don't know. I guess the whole Claire thing . . . now it feels awkward."

"It's only going to be awkward if you make it that way. Besides, I think she may have moved on. So moot point."

Right. Of course she had. She was dating that Jamie guy. What kind of stupid name was Jamie, anyway? It didn't matter. It wasn't like he was looking to jump into another relationship. He'd just gotten out of one. The right thing to do was take time off from dating. That would be easier if all his friends weren't married, but whatever. Still the right thing to do. "Yeah, okay. Why don't I run by the store and grab some ice cream or something?"

"Dee made cookies yesterday."

"Are they any good?"

Matt laughed. "I don't know. But I offered to bring dessert, too, and Jeremiah said Dee had it covered. I guess pregnancy is inspiring her to bake?"

That was almost terrifying. Deidre was a wizard with any sort of tool—hand tool, power tool, it didn't matter. But in the kitchen? That was not her forte. "I've been thinking about giving up sugar anyway."

Matt laughed. "That's almost word for word what Azure said. Maybe she'll surprise us."

Danny wasn't willing to bet on it, but he'd try to come up with something nice to say. "Okay. I'll catch you up there."

Danny headed to his car, stopping here and there to return a greeting and shake a hand. The small community church was always warm and welcoming. There were times when it was smothering, too. Small plus community tended to put everyone up in everyone else's business. But in the end, they meant well. Even Matt's aunt meant well, for all that she had a horrible way of showing it.

The drive up the mountain to Peacock Hill was relaxing. They were past the peak colors by several weeks, but even still some orange and gold leaves clung to trees. The branches wouldn't be completely bare until halfway through December. Mountains or no, they were still in the south and things stayed warmer longer.

Danny made the turn onto the driveway that wound up to the mansion. Making the final turn, he smiled as the house peeked out from behind the stand of cedars directly in front of it. Deidre had done something amazing with the place—she'd done the house and the town proud. And the steady trickle of visitors who came to events was helping keep some of the smaller businesses in town running. It was a good thing.

He parked behind Azure's truck and followed the sound of

laughter around the side of the house, through one of the sunken gardens, to the patio area in front of an enormous Romanesque fountain.

"Danny!" Deidre waved him over. "Matt said you were coming. I'm so glad."

He smiled and hooked his arm around her shoulders so he could give her a light squeeze. "It hasn't been all that long."

"I know. I just . . . Did he tell you I made cookies? Jeremiah's been warning people."

"I did hear about the cookies." Better to leave the whole "warning" thing alone. That was between her and her husband. Danny wasn't getting in the middle.

"Want to know a secret?" Deidre glanced around before leaning up on her tiptoes to whisper in his ear. "They're from a tube. I just cut and baked them."

Danny laughed, turning it into a cough when her elbow jabbed into his ribs.

"You can't say anything."

He mimed zipping his lips. This was going to be amusing. "How'd you hide the wrapper?"

Deidre gestured to her enormous belly. "The baby helped."

"Clever girl. Your secret's safe with me. You sure Jeremiah doesn't know?"

She shrugged. "I'm pretty sure he'd say something. You know Jer."

He did. And as much as he wanted to agree with Dee, he also suspected that his friend would go out of his way to set his wife up for success. Because the man was besotted. The two of them were creeping up on their first anniversary, with a baby due a few months after, and if anything they were more in love than ever. He patted Deidre's shoulder and stepped away, heading toward the grill.

His gaze skimmed the group. Jeremiah manned the giant,

stainless steel grill as it smoked and sizzled. Matt and Azure lounged in two folding chairs, their feet propped on the edge of the fountain, fingers laced together. Duncan and his wife, Anna, had stretched out on the ground nearby and the four of them were having a lively conversation. When Deidre approached, Duncan jumped to his feet and dragged another chair over so his sister could sit.

Where was Claire?

Danny pushed away the thought. Maybe she had other plans. That was okay. She had her own life, and he wasn't part of it.

But the rest of the group was.

"Smells good."

Jeremiah stopped stirring the strips of peppers and onion on a sheet pan that took up one side of the grill. "Hey, man. Wasn't sure you'd make it."

"Okay that I did?"

"Always. You know that."

"Just checking." Danny grinned. "Besides, you know I like these better than your nachos. If I know you're grilling skewers, I'm coming."

Jeremiah snickered. "I don't understand your aversion to nachos, but I guess I can let it slide. You hear about the cookies?"

"That Deidre baked? Yeah. Do we have an excuse ready in case they're inedible?" Even knowing they were from a tube didn't completely erase Danny's suspicion of the treats. Deidre and the kitchen were simply not a combination he was going to take without a lot of caution.

"They're good. I snuck one last night—couldn't sleep. Honestly, man, they're nearly the same as the ones Matt's aunt makes. I'm impressed."

Danny nodded, fighting not to laugh. At least Deidre hadn't messed up scoop and bake cookies. He wouldn't have put it past her. "All right, then I guess I'm looking forward to it."

"That's the spirit. You need a drink? I think Duncan set up a tub with some sodas."

"I'm good for now. Can I help?"

"Nah. It's almost ready. You figure out what you're doing about Casey yet?"

Danny sighed. "I drove up yesterday—figured why put it off, you know? We're done."

"Yeah?" Jeremiah slapped Danny on the back. "Good for you. You okay?"

"I guess. It's not fun. She cried. Then she started yelling— maybe some of what she said was right. I don't know."

"Like what?" Jeremiah reached under the grill for a platter and started loading finished kabobs onto it.

He shrugged. "That I led her on, made her think we were heading toward something more serious when I'd really only been goofing around. That sort of thing."

"That's a tough one. Here," Jeremiah shoved the platter at Danny, "take that over to the table and tell people it's ready, would you?"

"Yeah." Was that the end of the conversation about Casey? Not exactly as helpful as he would've liked. Whatever. He knew he'd done the right thing—or he mostly knew that. Casey'd get over it. "Where's Claire?"

Jeremiah chuckled. "Why don't you give her a call and see?"

Danny shook his head and carried the food to the picnic table that sat close to the portico at the back of the house. He caught Duncan's eye and gestured toward the food. Duncan nodded and soon the rest of the group was headed over, still chatting.

"Did someone call Claire?" Deidre slid onto the bench at one end and stopped, her baby bump preventing her from scooting along to make room for more people. "Sorry guys, you'll have to step in. The whale is stuck."

Jeremiah chuckled and kissed her head. "You're beautiful. And that's what we'd do anyway. Danny was going to call Claire."

Conversation stopped and everyone turned to look at Danny.

Heat crawled up his neck. He glared at Jeremiah and tugged his phone out of his pocket. Opening a message, he let Claire know lunch was ready out back. "There. Happy?"

Jeremiah shook his head and sat next to his wife. "Sure. What about you?"

Danny frowned and took a seat. What was that supposed to mean? He wasn't here to jump into a relationship with Claire. She wasn't even available anymore.

Was he happy? He didn't know how to approach the question to find an answer.

7

M onday morning, Claire smoothed the comforter on the bed in the room where she'd grown up and glanced around. Her parents hadn't changed it much since she moved out. Mom had taken down the posters of Christian bands that Claire had hung in high school, but her knickknacks and trophies still lined the shelves and dresser top.

Raised voices reached her from downstairs. They weren't loud enough to make out the words, but the tone made her cringe. Should she go down or stay up here until they stopped? She really didn't want to get in the middle of her parents arguing. They didn't fight often, but when they did . . . she shook her head and sank to the edge of the bed.

Claire checked her phone. There was still plenty of time.

She'd just wait here.

She scrolled through her various social media feeds, trying desperately to ignore the voices that pitched louder and harsher from downstairs. Finally, she clicked off her phone and closed her eyes. They weren't going to stop.

A deep breath and she stood. She could do this. And maybe her presence would remind her parents they weren't alone in the house right now. Not that that was comforting. If they were fighting like this when she was home, what did they do when she wasn't?

It had to be a fluke. Didn't it?

Claire made her way downstairs and into the kitchen. She took a mug down from the cabinet and reached for the coffee pot.

". . . and for another thing," her mother swept into the kitchen. Claire's gaze met her mom's and her mom smiled. "Oh, hello sweetie. How did you sleep?"

Claire blinked. "Um. Okay I guess. Everything all right?"

Why had she asked? What was she thinking? Obviously nothing was all right and she didn't really want to know the details she'd missed trying to hide in her room.

"Of course, of course. Just a little disagreement because your father is an imbecile."

"I heard that!" Claire's dad strode into the room and shot a glare at her mom. He edged around the counter and kissed Claire's cheek. "Morning, baby. I'm sorry your mother's a shrew. Hopefully it's not catching."

"Dad." Shock won over silence and Claire stared at her parents. "What is going on? All this name calling? Over what? Seriously, what started this?"

"Your mother moved the TV remote. Again. After I specifically asked her to leave it on the arm of the couch."

"It's irritating when it's there. Honestly, how hard is it to find in the drawer of the end table? Then it's not visible and it's not always falling off onto the floor. Is it really so hard to remember and make a few extra movements before your sedentary butt lands in its wallow for the day?"

"Sedentary? Wallow?" Dad turned his furious gaze on Claire. "Do you hear this? I have put up with her insults for thirty-five years, and it's getting old."

"Then why don't you just leave?" Her mother's voice moved back into a shout as she crossed her arms.

"Because it's my house. If you're so unhappy, why don't *you* leave?" Dad mimicked her pose.

"You know what? I think I will." Mom stormed from the room and stomped up the stairs. The sound of drawers and doors banging carried into the otherwise silent kitchen.

"Dad?"

He waved a hand in front of him. "Don't worry about it. She's not going anywhere. Not once she realizes she can't afford to live in the manner to which she's become accustomed."

Claire looked at the mug of coffee and slowly set it in the sink. Her stomach was twisted into knots and every muscle teetered on the edge of shaking. "You're just going to let her go? Why don't you apologize? Fix things?"

"What's the point? It's the TV remote today. Tomorrow it'll be a banana peel or something else just as stupid. It's only prolonging the inevitable."

"The inevitable?" Claire's mouth was dust. "What are you saying?"

"She wants a divorce. Has for, oh, eight or nine months now. Frankly, I'm getting tired of fighting her. Maybe it's time to let her have her way."

"But you said she'd be back? You're not really going to get divorced."

He sank into a seat at the kitchen table. "Maybe, maybe not. I guess we'll see. If it's still what she wants, then I guess I might as well go along with it. She won't take me up on any of the things I've suggested to try and fix it."

Claire battled the tears that burned her eyes. "You can't— that's not—why?"

Dad just shrugged.

Right. Okay. She took a deep breath. Then another. It only

served to make her dizzy. "I—I need to go. I don't think I'll be staying all week after all."

"Oh, sweetie. Don't let your mother's craziness push you away."

"Dad." Claire clamped her lips shut. If her father couldn't see that he was every bit as much to blame as her mother, that was his problem. She was not going to be able to change his mind in the fifteen minutes she had before she needed to leave for her first interview.

She pressed a hand to her stomach and headed back upstairs. She'd pack up and go. If she had to get a hotel, she would, but she still had some friends in the area. Maybe one of them would let her couch surf until Wednesday.

A three-day interview process seemed extreme, especially when Jamie assured her it was a formality, but it was what the company did.

With her suitcase packed—including a few things from her room that she didn't want to lose if her parents lost their minds more than they already had—Claire hurried downstairs. At the front door, she paused and looked down the central hall of the house where she'd grown up. Was this the last time she'd be here with both parents and the family she'd always known?

She swallowed and blinked back tears. *Don't think about it. Just go.*

She called out, "Bye!"

Pulling the door shut behind her had a finality about it that she couldn't quite wrap her mind around.

What was she supposed to do now?

"I REALLY APPRECIATE THIS." Claire pushed her suitcase over

beside the wall and wrung her hands. "I can get a hotel if I'm in the way."

"You're not in the way." Louisiana Carter laughed and tugged Claire into the living room. "Any friend of Nick's is welcome any time."

"More a sister of a friend of Nick's. It's a tenuous connection at best."

"Pshaw." Louisiana shook her head. "Nick says he knew you, too. He did tune your piano, right?"

Claire nodded. This had been her last resort before looking for a hotel room. Duncan and Nick had been friends when Duncan lived up here. Claire sort of knew the guy, but not super well. Texting Duncan to see if it was a good idea had been hard —she hadn't wanted to call on the off chance the situation with her parents came up. She didn't want to get into it. Not with Duncan. Certainly not with Deidre. It was going to be hard enough to explain why she was in DC in the first place. She wasn't touching the mess of her folks.

Regardless, Duncan had touched base with Nick and his wife Louisiana and now, here Claire was. The woman was chattering at her and she'd missed it all.

"I'm sorry." Claire bit her lip. "I—"

"Oh, *cher*, don't worry about it." Louisiana's southern drawl thickened. "You're probably exhausted after a day of interviews. Sit. Let me get you some sweet tea. Nick should be home any minute. They needed him at the Kennedy Center today. He doesn't usually have time to tune—not anymore. But we're taking a little breather from composing and recording until after Thanksgiving. YouTube will survive without us for a couple of weeks."

Right. Duncan had told her that Nick and Louisiana spent most of their time now filming videos for original piano compositions. The two of them were quite the sensation in the online indie music world and were in negotiations for an album contract. They toured—a lot—as well, which was a wonder giving Nick's problem with stage fright. "Thanks. When do you go back on the road?"

"We're doing some Christmas shows in December on the Eastern Seaboard. Then we'll do another US and Europe tour starting in February. I'm excited to spend a week or so with Nick's family in Tuscany while we're over there. His Nonna has remarried, and her new husband is a gem." Louisiana disappeared through a doorway, returning a few minutes later with two tall glasses of iced tea. "I guess I should have offered something hot. Would you prefer that?"

"This is fine, really." Claire took the tea and sipped, her eyes widening. "That's sweet."

Louisiana laughed. "Sorry. Nick says I need to warn people. It's simple syrup added when the tea's hot. Good, Southern sweet tea. I can get you something else."

"No, no, it's good. I was surprised is all." Claire took another sip before setting the glass on the coffee table. "Do you like this area?"

"Well enough. It's close to DC. There's almost everything we need within walking distance if we want." Louisiana shrugged. "Why do you ask?"

"Oh. Thinking out loud. If I get this job then I'd move up here. Moving back would mean I need a place to live." Claire shrugged. She hadn't given that much thought previously. Her parents had always said any of their children could come home and stay—but now? Even if the invitation stood, Claire wasn't going back. She also wasn't thinking about it anymore. Her stomach was starting to hurt again.

"It'd be fun to be neighbors. I've heard so much about your family from Nick—I guess he's known your brother a long time."

"Yeah. He has." Where was she supposed to go with that? It

was another reminder that Nick and Duncan were friends. Claire was just the little sister. Should she have gotten a hotel? She was intruding. "I—"

"You must be tired. Why don't we take your bag into the guest room and you can get settled, collect your thoughts. And if you want to stay in there all evening, that's fine too. Don't feel like you have to hang out with us, but we'd love it if you'd join us for dinner." Louisiana stood and crossed to the door to snag Claire's suitcase by its handle. "I'll apologize now for the state of the second bedroom. It's small and full of recording equipment. But the bed is comfortable. Just move whatever you need to."

Claire followed Louisiana down a hallway and waited while she pushed open a door. Full of equipment was an understatement. It was organized, at least, but the shelving that lined three of the four walls was stacked with boxes and bins. A daybed occupied the fourth wall, positioned under the window that was covered with blinds and nothing else.

"Is it okay?"

"It's great. Thanks again for letting me crash. I'll head back on Wednesday, so it's just tonight and tomorrow."

"If things go long on Wednesday and you want to stay here again and leave Thursday morning, the door's open. Just let us know."

"Thanks." Claire hit a button on her phone as it started to buzz.

"I'll let you get that. Come out if you need anything or want some company." Louisiana gave a little wave and left, pulling the door closed behind her.

Claire sank onto the bed and tapped her phone. She checked the call log. Her parents had both been calling her all day. She'd ignored them. She was not getting involved in their madness. But this most recent call was Jamie. Her lips curved and she tapped to return the call. She settled back against the pillows as it rang.

"Hey. That was fast."

"That's me. Super speedy." Claire chuckled. "It's the first call I've gotten today that I wanted to answer."

"Spam? I get so much of that. It's crazy. Hang on." Claire heard a little rustling and a thump before Jamie was back on the line. "There. Door's closed. How did today go?"

He was still at work? It was after five, and she knew he'd been at the office before seven. "Good, I guess. I don't have a lot of experience with interviews. So I either nailed it, or I bombed and am clueless. I'm not sure which. I don't guess you've heard one way or the other?"

"That'd be cheating, wouldn't it?" The fact that he was grinning showed in his voice. "Come to dinner with me, though, and I might be persuaded to give you some details."

"Jamie . . ." Was it smart to go to dinner with him? If she got the job, could she still date the boss? What if she didn't get it? Or decided not to take it? "Aren't you even a little worried about how complicated this could get?"

"How is dinner complicated? You eat and talk. No strings, I promise."

She needed to eat. She'd only picked at her lunch. And breakfast, well, her parents had wrecked that. "Yeah, okay. Where can I meet you?"

"Why don't I pick you up?"

Because that made it feel even more like a date. Because it meant she couldn't leave if it did start to get awkward and complicated. Any reason she thought up sounded lame inside her head. And after living at Peacock Hill for the past almost two years, not driving in the insanity of DC area traffic was a bonus. "All right. Thanks."

"Where do your parents live?"

"Oh. Right. I'm actually at a friend of my brother's. Things at home were—this is just better." She rattled off the address.

"Give me about an hour?"

"Sure. I'll wait out front. See you in a bit." Claire ended the call and frowned. Was she supposed to dress up? Well, she couldn't, so that was that. She'd suggest someplace casual when he got here. Casual and nearby.

That would help it feel less like a date, too.

If she got the job, she wanted it to be on her own merits. Not because Jamie was angling to get her to move closer so they could explore a relationship. Did she even want that? She needed to get over the idea of Danny—move on—but was jumping into something with Jamie the best way to do that?

It didn't seem fair to him.

Or to Danny.

8

"You coming up for movie night?"

Claire looked up from her computer and rubbed her eyes. "Huh?"

Danny chuckled. She looked so cute and studious. Not that he was noticing cute on anyone. "Movie night. Upstairs? It's Friday. You know that, right?"

"Right."

"Deidre said she told you this morning. I think they decided on Die Hard." It was an oldie but a goodie as far as he was concerned. Explosions. Triumph of the underdog. What's not to love? "Start off the Christmas season with a bang."

Claire tipped her head to the side. "You're not seriously one of the weirdoes who consider Die Hard a Christmas movie."

"What's to consider? Where is it set?" He raised his eyebrows and fought a laugh as she visibly struggled with her answer.

"An office party."

"What kind of office party?"

"Fine. An office Christmas party. But that doesn't make it a Christmas movie."

"Really? Interesting." Danny dropped into one of the visitor chairs across the desk from Claire and crossed his legs. "Tell me more."

"It just isn't. There's no possible way that happening to be set at a Christmas party makes it a Christmas movie. If you made it a retirement party, the whole thing would still work."

"I beg to differ. McClain wouldn't be out there for a retirement party."

Claire sighed. "Please. He wanted to reconcile with his wife. If she asked him to come, he'd come."

"What about the whole 'Ho, ho, ho, now I have a machine gun' part? That makes no sense without it being a *Christmas* movie." He leaned back. That made his point. Firmly. And it had put some color in her cheeks. Something that had been missing when he'd entered the tiny office.

"Well, sure, they included a few things because again, set during the season, but they could've made a retirement joke instead. Christmas has nothing to do with the plot. It's set at Christmas. It's not a Christmas movie. But," she held up a finger, "since it's not even Thanksgiving yet, it's still an appropriate choice. If we were past Thanksgiving though, I'd have to consider it a party foul."

"Party foul? It's an amazing movie. Why would it be a foul?"

Claire clicked the mouse a few times before pushing back from the desk. "Because from Thanksgiving to Christmas—possibly New Year's Eve—you can only watch Christmas movies."

Danny shook his head. "Where is that written down?"

"Everyone knows this. It doesn't have to be written down." She brushed past him.

His nerve endings tingled. Had she always had this effect on him and he hadn't noticed? It didn't seem possible. Danny hit the lights and followed her to the stairs. "I still think it counts as a Christmas movie."

Claire patted his shoulder. "Go ahead and hold on to that. You're wrong, but you're committed to it. That shows strength of character."

He snorted and held open the stairwell door. "I could say the same about you."

"Whatever." Claire started up the steps.

"Why weren't you at dinner?" He followed behind her and frowned. Was she losing weight? He wasn't going to ask—that was a no-win situation. But maybe he'd keep an eye on her—she didn't need to get any skinnier than she already was.

"Wasn't in the mood for pizza. I'll grab something later."

"How about I make some popcorn? Extra butter, the way you like it?"

Claire reached the top of the stairs and spun, jabbing her finger into his shoulder. "What's with you? Why are you being so nice? Why are you even here? You should be on a date with Casey."

He ignored the clutch around his heart as her eyes filled and grabbed the finger that was still poking him. "Casey and I broke up. You guys are my friends—you, especially—and I've missed hanging out here. I was told I was welcome any time. What's going on, Claire?"

She shook her head. "Leave it alone. I'm sorry I jabbed you."

"Pfft. Please. You poke like a girl."

"I am a girl."

"There you are, then." He smiled slightly when she rolled her eyes. "If you weren't okay, would you tell me?"

She stared at him. "No. I don't think I would."

Ouch. Danny swallowed. "Well. Tell someone, okay?"

Claire shrugged.

Danny frowned. Words clashed against one another in his head, but he pushed them back and clamped his lips together. A lecture never did any good. In this case, it'd probably make things worse. He scooted around her, careful not to brush against her—the very last thing he needed was the electrifying reminder of what she could do to him—and headed for the kitchen.

He'd make some popcorn.

If Claire didn't want any, he'd eat it himself.

"I'm surprised to see you in today, Danny. Thought you'd take the whole week off." Martin looked out over the mostly deserted office space. "Seems to be the thing to do this year."

"I'm not traveling for Thanksgiving, and there's plenty to do. You're in."

Martin laughed. "So I am. Same reasons. My wife wanted me to take the week—pushed hard for it, actually—but she's going to be cleaning and cooking all week and I didn't want to get dragged into that."

"You have family coming in?" There was plenty to do. That wasn't a lie, but Danny could take a few minutes to show his boss he was interested and a team player.

"All the kids—four of 'em. Two are married, so wives as well. And then the apple of my eye, our first granddaughter. Have you seen her?" Martin offered his phone.

Danny looked down at the angelic smiling face of a toddler —he had no idea how old she was. Kid ages were a mystery. "She's beautiful."

"She's my doll baby, that's the truth. Almost two and so precocious. Of course, her mother says I spoil her, but isn't that my job? And honestly, I'd like to see the man who can resist those brown eyes." Martin smiled lovingly at the picture before putting away his phone. "I just had a call from Gerry. He's very pleased with the changes you made to his plans. He wanted to be sure I knew you were doing exceptional work."

"Oh, that's great to know. I was going to follow up with Mr. Robertson this afternoon. I had an idea for the second floor study. We could cantilever a balcony off the west side. I overheard his wife talking about wanting a greenhouse, and while this would still be part of the house, it might be enough to scratch that itch for her."

"Hm. They don't have the yard space. That's what Gerry's always saying when she gets on her greenhouse kick. Isn't southern exposure best?"

"Depends. Sometimes south gets too much sun. You end up needing to provide shades. Their exposure isn't due west. I really think it'd get plenty of light."

Martin nodded. "Run it by him. You might just be the hero of the day. That's the kind of initiative I like to see. Good job, Danny."

"Thank you." That was a relief. He'd been on the fence about mentioning it. The greenhouse conversation had happened in the background, so it hadn't been meant for his ears. But if Martin thought it was worth mentioning, then the greenhouse debate must be a fairly common occurrence for the Robertsons. He didn't see the excitement of having dirt under his fingernails, but whatever. Everyone needed a hobby. "I was thinking I'd call it sort of a conservatory rather than a greenhouse since it's part of the living space."

"Oh, Sheila will like that. It sounds fancy. She's someone who's impressed by stuff like that. But if you say that to anyone, I'll deny it furiously."

Danny grinned. "Your secret's safe with me."

"I shouldn't give her grief. She's the reason we have their business in the first place. She about nagged Gerry to death until he finally asked me to get some proposals put together. It's the little things—like this new idea of a conservatory—that put yours clearly on the top of the pile." Martin paused and glanced in the direction of Sly's cube. "He give you any more trouble?"

"No, sir." Not that Danny would admit it even if that wasn't the case. No one ever succeeded in the business place by running to their boss about annoying coworkers.

"You tell me if he does. I mean it. There are other issues at play, and I'd value your input."

Danny pressed his lips together and nodded slowly. He didn't want to be a tattler. But if his boss told him to . . . it was good to do as you were told. "Yes, sir."

Martin cocked his head to the side. "There's something."

Danny frowned. "He's just always standing up, looking around at what everyone else is doing. It's not a problem, really."

"But it's annoying. And why does it matter to him? I'll take care of it. That's exactly what I need to know."

"Okay. Um. I guess he's also always telling people to send him their stuff and he'll go over it. He always sounds like he's offering to be helpful, but people like Marsha have a hard time saying no."

"Interesting." Martin drummed his fingers on the top of Danny's cube wall. "I might have an idea about that. Let me think on it some. I might need your help down the road."

"Okay."

"Anything else?"

Was there? Those were the big issues that made Sly a constant—or semi-constant—annoyance. He shook his head. "Not really."

"Keep me posted. I'll let you get back to it. Good call on the conservatory. I think Gerry's going to be pleased. Have you already worked up a plan?"

"Just a sketch to try and get the idea solidified. See how it would work. It's nothing formal."

"Good enough. Gerry's visual—which you probably already figured out from having to deal with him." Martin chuckled. "Shoot him that sketch maybe twenty minutes before you call. That'll give him time to think about it and show Sheila."

He'd planned to offer to send it after floating the idea, but he could do it the other way around. Martin knew his friends better than Danny did. "Will do. Thanks."

Martin made his signature knock on the top of the cube wall before meandering down the aisle toward his office.

Danny swiveled back to his computer monitor and wiggled the mouse. He really should tidy up that sketch if the client was going to see it before he had a chance to walk through the idea with him.

He checked the clock. There was time. Thanksgiving week was a laid back week.

DANNY COLLECTED his gyro and fries from the pickup counter and turned. The spices mingling in the air had his mouth watering as he scanned the room for an empty table.

"Hey, Danny."

Danny froze. Casey. He knew better than to come here on a Monday. Casey always wanted gyros on Monday. Forcing a smile and praying it was casual, he glanced over. "Hi, Casey. How's it going?"

"Really? That's what you're going with?"

The scent of the food was no longer tantalizing. Instead of the heady mix of spices, the only scent he could pick out was the grease. His stomach knotted. "Apparently. What would you have preferred?"

She propped her fists on her hips. "Why are you in here?"

"Because I wanted a gyro and it's lunch time and I can walk

here from the office." All of which were reasons they used to meet here nearly every Monday for lunch. He wasn't thinking about Casey. He hadn't been thinking about her since they broke things off. Which, okay, was a great confirmation that breaking up was the right thing to do, but it didn't keep him out of situations like this. "Do you want to join me?"

"Join you? No, I don't want to join you. I don't think you should come in here. Ever."

"You can't ban me from a restaurant, Casey. You don't get the gyro place in our breakup."

"I don't see why I shouldn't. I introduced you to it. You can wind out the whole 'within easy walking distance' spiel if you want, but the reality is you never came here until I suggested it."

He sighed. "You're right. Thank you for introducing me to the best gyros in the area. And so conveniently located for me, too. Unlike you, who have to drive across town to get here."

"What's that supposed to mean? You think I came here just to see you? Like I somehow knew you were heading here?" She scowled at him before turning to collect her food from the window.

"Did you?"

Red washed over her cheeks and she looked away.

"Seriously, Casey?"

She shrugged.

"So, what? You came here to pick a fight? What's the point of that? We already broke up—what's the end game beyond that?" Danny shook his head. "Whatever. Enjoy your food. That's what I'm going to go do."

"Don't walk away from me."

Danny kept going across the restaurant. He found a tiny table for two and slid into the seat with his back to the wall. He hooked the other chair with his foot and dragged it closer so he could prop his knee on it.

Casey stared at him before marching to his table and slamming down her tray. "I've changed my mind. I will join you."

"Sorry. Offer's rescinded."

She jerked on the chair until she freed it and sat.

What was she doing? More to the point, why? Asking would only encourage it though. That much was obvious. So he'd ignore her. He could manage that. He was tempted to pack up his food and eat at his desk, but that seemed like giving in. He had arrived first. He was going to eat here, like he'd planned originally.

Casey wasn't going to chase him off.

Danny picked up his gyro and bit in. He could remember how it should taste—juicy and exotic—but today it might as well have been dust. He shot up a quick prayer for wisdom. Was he supposed to say something?

Her stare burned into the top of his head, but he refused to look up. It felt childish, but he didn't see the point in being even more of a public spectacle than they'd already become.

She sighed loudly.

Danny dunked french fries into his tzatziki.

Casey cleared her throat.

He swallowed and reached for his soda. She grabbed his hand.

Danny jerked his hand away and frowned at her.

"Danny." Casey's eyes filled. "I don't understand. I need you to help me understand."

That did it. His appetite was gone. His ability to pretend to eat had also vanished. Danny flipped the lid of the container shut and blew out a breath. "I told you before, Casey, this just isn't going to work. I suspected when we started dating and I knew after a couple of weeks. I tried to convince myself it didn't matter that we didn't have our faith in common—you were always respectful, which I appreciate. But I was starting to compromise my beliefs because it would make things easier between us. I can't do that. It's not fair to either of us."

"You realize how stupid that sounds, right?"

He shrugged and stood. "It doesn't sound stupid to me. I'm sorry it does to you. I can't be who you want me to be and be who Jesus expects me to be at the same time. I'll try to remember not to crave gyros on Mondays, okay? See you around, Casey."

"Danny..."

He kept walking. He slid on his sunglasses as he stepped out into the brisk November afternoon. He probably should've worn a jacket. There was enough of a nip to the air that he'd be chilled when he reached the office.

Maybe concentrating on that would keep his mind off the fact that the woman he didn't want wouldn't leave him alone. The woman he did want? She didn't even want to be friends anymore.

He couldn't fix either situation.

9

Claire dumped the boiled potatoes into the bowl of her mixer and lowered the beaters. She dumped in a chunk of butter and splashed in some cream. People could make potatoes however they wanted, but this was what her mother had taught her.

Her mother.

Claire ignored her churning stomach and started the mixer. She still hadn't said anything to Deidre or Duncan. Neither had pushed. Of course, she hadn't explained why she'd headed back to DC in the first place. She already knew how the job interview conversation was going to go over with Deidre. Claire didn't need her sister going into premature labor.

Duncan might get it. He'd left a prestigious job in DC to start his own company down here. So sure, the entrepreneurial spirit ran strong in him. But he'd also enjoyed working for someone else's firm. Realistically, without a few bad apples there, he'd still be doing that. So maybe he'd understand where Claire was coming from.

Claire turned on the mixer and watched as the potatoes whirled into creamy goodness. She also had cranberry sauce to make. That was the sum total of her contribution to Thanksgiving this year. Deidre had wanted to do the rest and only let go of the potatoes because Claire kept nagging. Anna and Azure had offered to bring something and been shut down—although Azure would probably just bring something anyway. She was like that.

She switched off the potatoes and frowned. Someone was banging on her apartment door. Wiping her hands on a towel, she crossed through the living room and tugged the door open.

"Mom."

Her mother smiled and started to step into the room. "Hi, honey."

"What are you doing here?"

Eyebrows arched, Claire's mom shot her an enquiring look. "Do I get to come in?"

"I guess." Claire stepped back and, when her mother was through the door, looked into the hallway. Empty. She wasn't going to ask where Dad was, even though she itched to know. "So?"

"Your father and I came down to have Thanksgiving with our children. Deidre invited us several weeks ago."

That sounded like her sister. To be fair, prior to Claire's recent trip up there, it would also have sounded like her. "Ah."

"That's it?"

"What do you want me to say, Mom?"

"You haven't said anything to your siblings."

It wasn't a question. Claire shrugged. "Not my place."

Her mother sighed and looked away. "I guess it was too much to hope for."

"Which means . . .?"

"I guess your father and I were hoping the initial shock would have worn off by now and we could approach this holiday under the guise of the new normal."

"You're not going to tell them on Thanksgiving. You can't possibly be that . . ." Words failed her. Stupid? Cruel? Insensitive?

"You're all together. It actually seemed like the perfect time."

"With friends in attendance?"

Her mother waved away the objection. "Please. Matt and Azure hardly count. It's not as if filling them in wouldn't be first on everyone's agenda anyway."

"And Danny?"

"Is he going to be here?" Her mother lifted one shoulder. "I suppose that makes sense. And as he's in the same camp as Matt when it comes to your brother-in-law—practically family—I don't see why not. We signed a separation agreement on Friday, it's time everyone knew."

"Mom. You can't do this on Thanksgiving." A hot, heavy ball settled in Claire's stomach.

"You can't expect me to pretend that everything's the way it's always been. I'm done with that. I had too many years of—"

"Stop. Just stop. I'm not getting in the middle of this. If you and Dad go through with a divorce, as far as I'm concerned, you're both dead to me."

"Claire."

"Don't act shocked and injured. You're not spending even five minutes thinking about what your selfish behavior is going to do to your kids."

"Of course you take his side." Her mother sniffed. "I should have known."

"I'm not taking anyone's side. If Dad's letting you do this, he's just as wrong as you. Now get out. If you're going to insist on ruining Thanksgiving, I obviously can't stop you, but I won't be a party to it." She managed to keep her voice from betraying her, but the desperate need to sob clawed at her throat and burned her eyes.

Her mother frowned at her for three long heartbeats before jerking her chin into the air and storming out of the apartment. The door slammed.

Claire sank to the floor and buried her face in her hands as the sobs ripped through her.

～

"I don't understand."

Claire frowned at Deidre. "What's to understand? I don't feel well. Here are the potatoes and the cranberry sauce."

"You cooked even though you're sick?" Deidre tipped her head to the side. "What's going on?"

Claire just shook her head. She didn't want to get into it. Let her parents be the ones who ruined everything. It wasn't her job. "Nothing, okay? Can you just take the food?"

"Will you come up and sit with us? If your stomach is hurting, you don't have to eat, but I know Mom and Dad—"

"Dee, please. Can you drop it? Take the food. I don't want to come up there and watch everyone eat. I want to go back to bed." Maybe, if she pulled the covers over her head for long enough, she could pretend the underpinnings of her life weren't shattering.

"This isn't over." Deidre scooped up the bowl of mashed potatoes, hugging it in the crook of her arm, and picked up the smaller dish of cranberries. "I'll save you pie."

Claire managed a small smile. Pie was the best part of Thanksgiving. "Okay. Thanks."

Deidre disappeared through Claire's apartment door and Claire flipped the lock. Knowing her sister, it was possible Duncan would show up fishing for an explanation next. Or Anna. Deidre was bound to send someone. Then what?

At some point, Claire wouldn't be able to hold in the words.

She didn't want to do her mother's dirty work for her. She wasn't going to be responsible for setting someone else off on the tailspin she found herself in.

She climbed into her bed fully dressed, tugged the comforter up over her shoulders, and closed her eyes. Claire wanted to pray. But what was she supposed to say? Where had God been *before* her parents were at the point of hiring lawyers and signing separation agreements? That sounded so final. A separation agreement. Did that mean they were already divorced?

Rolling over, Claire fumbled for her phone and opened a web browser. A few quick searches revealed more about Virginia divorce law than she'd ever figured she'd need to know. But at least she knew her parents were still married.

For now.

Since Claire and her siblings were all adults, her parents only had to wait six months before they could file and finalize the dissolution of their family.

Even if God was interested in intervening, was that enough time?

Oh sure, He could work miracles. If He wanted to. But seriously, when was the last time God was visibly involved in any part of her life? She prayed. She went to church. She did all the things Christians were supposed to do, and what happened? Maybe God protected her from getting run over when she was crossing the street, but she couldn't nail down anything more that she could absolutely chalk up to Him.

If God wanted to show up, now would be a great time.

Preferably before her parents shared the news and officially shattered the foundation of everything her siblings took for granted.

Tap tap tap.

Claire rolled over and pried her eyes open. She blinked. What time was it? She wiggled until she was half-sitting and reached for her phone . . . which was not on her nightstand. She must have fallen asleep while she was looking at it. She tossed the covers and it clattered to the floor.

Fantastic.

With her luck these days, the screen was probably broken.

The tapping continued.

Claire threw her legs over the side of the bed and stood. She scooped up the phone as she shuffled to the door of her apartment and pulled it open.

"What?"

Danny offered a tentative smile. "I wanted to check on you."

"Still alive, as you see. Thanks." She started to close the door. Danny braced his hand against it.

"Claire."

She sighed. "What?"

"Can I come in?"

Why? What was the point? From the look on his face it was obvious that her parents had gone ahead with their ridiculous and horrific announcement. Then again, Danny wasn't going to slink off just because she gave him attitude. He'd proven that more times than she could count over the course of their relationship. "Whatever."

Claire stalked into the kitchen and pulled down a mug from her cupboard. She glanced over her shoulder and watched as Danny carefully closed the door behind him and tucked his hands in the pockets of his khakis. He'd dressed up a little for Thanksgiving. The burgundy sweater went well with his eyes. A little of the ice around her heart thawed. "I'm making tea. You want some?"

He wrinkled his nose. "I guess. But not that flowery stuff."

She smiled and reached for another mug. She had actually been thinking of chamomile, but it was easy enough to switch to something else. After a nap, it wasn't like she'd get to bed at her usual time anyway, so if she went with a black tea, the difference would be negligible. "Earl Grey?"

"I guess. It's good enough for Picard, right?"

"Only you, Danny." How he watched hours of that ancient Star Trek was beyond her. She'd watched a few episodes with him—well, not with him, it happened to be on while she was in the room. For a space show, it wasn't awful. She turned on the burner under her kettle and scooped tea into the teapot.

"I take it you'd already talked to your parents?"

There it was. Danny wasn't one to beat around the bush.

"I was up last week, remember? It was obvious."

He nodded and leaned back against the counter. "How are you?"

"I don't know. I can't wrap my head around it. Every time I tell myself I'm going to sit and really think about what this means, I can't. I just can't go there."

"So you take a nap?"

She shrugged. "Today I did. Should you be leaving Casey up there by herself? That has to be awkward for her."

"Nice try. I told you we broke up."

"Figured maybe you'd gotten over that."

He stared at her.

She hunched her shoulders. "What? It happens."

The kettle began to whistle. Claire flicked off the stove and poured the boiling water into the teapot.

"Not this time. God finally got through to me. Thankfully before I made any decisions that were even harder to undo." Danny paused. He held up a finger. "Hang on. Is this what was bothering you on Friday? Your parents?"

Of course he'd remember that. She gave a short nod.

"Why didn't you say anything?"

"What was I supposed to say? My parents are getting a divorce." The word caught in her throat and her eyes filled. She wrapped her arms around herself and rocked. "Everything I grew up believing is a lie."

"No." Danny crossed the small kitchen and pulled her into his arms. She stood stiff, even as the warmth from him soaked soothingly into her. "No, baby, that's not what it means."

"How do you know? How can you possibly understand?"

He brushed his lips across her forehead. "My parents split when I was nine."

Claire shook her head. "No. I've met your mom. And your dad. Together."

"Stepmom, technically. Dad remarried when I was fourteen. Mom hasn't. She doesn't keep in touch—an email at Christmas, the occasional text. She moved to California—seems happy enough out there from the little she tells me. But I can absolutely promise you two things that I spent a lot of years in therapy trying to internalize. One, it's not your fault or responsibility. And two, everything you believed growing up about your parents was true at the time. People change. Not always for the better."

Claire dropped her forehead to Danny's shoulder and sifted through his words. She hadn't considered that it was her fault—so that wasn't an issue. What did it say about her that she hadn't gone there? Probably nothing. But the other . . . could it be true? "I don't know if that's any better. Either everything I believed about how much they loved each other was a lie or they changed so much that their love turned into disgust for one another. I don't really like either choice."

Danny stroked her back in gentle circles. "I know. I get that."

She took a deep, shuddering breath. Why hadn't she wanted to talk to someone? Why had she kept this to herself? Telling

Danny had eased a tiny bit of the tightness around her heart. Being in his arms—even if it was simply because he was offering comfort and didn't mean anything else—was bittersweet. She relaxed a little more and slipped her arms loosely around his waist. "Thanks, Danny."

He rested his cheek on her head. "Anytime. It's what friends do."

Friends. Right. Claire eased back and tipped up her face to smile at him. When her gaze met his, she swallowed. There was something in his eyes that spoke of more than friendship. Or she was projecting. Seeing what she wanted to see even if it wasn't there.

"Claire . . ." Danny squeezed his eyes shut. "I should—"

"Don't go yet. Please? We could watch something? And there's the tea."

"There's something you should know first."

He was going to give her the "we're just friends" speech. Because of course he automatically assumed that she was throwing herself at him. Well, she wasn't. That part of her life was over. She was working on getting over him, wasn't she? She'd been on a handful of dates with Jamie Fisher and one of these days, if she kept at it long enough, she was going to start feeling something for the guy. Bracing herself, she tried for a casual smile. "What's that?"

Danny studied her and drew in a breath like he was about to speak. He stopped, shook his head slightly, and his arms tightened around her a fraction of a second before his mouth lowered to hers.

Claire froze. Then she melted into his kiss. At the back of her mind, a tiny voice whispered that this wasn't going to help her get over Danny.

She ignored it. It wasn't as if that was really going to happen anyway.

10

W hat had he been thinking, kissing Claire?

The question had kept him up most of the night, but he was no closer to an answer than he'd been when he finally got home last night.

Of course, they hadn't stopped with one kiss. Claire had gone on to pour the tea and they'd snuggled in on her couch, finally settling on kicking off the Christmas movie season with White Christmas.

Not usually his favorite—Bing Crosby was fine, but he preferred Holiday Inn if he was forced to watch a movie with singing and dancing in it. Still, this viewing was several large steps up in his estimation when he compared it to any of the times he'd watched it before.

His mom and sister did not compare to Claire.

She'd sung along and hadn't seemed to care that she was off key.

His phone buzzed with an incoming text. Danny sighed and rolled out of bed, grabbing the phone on his way into the kitchen. If he wasn't going to sleep, he could make coffee and pretend to work.

When the single cup machine was brewing, he tapped the phone and opened his messages.

Jeremiah.

Why wasn't he surprised?

You up?

Danny tapped back an affirmative and reached for his mug.

Someone pounded on the door.

Leaving his coffee, Danny went to open it.

Jeremiah held out a box of doughnuts. "I come bearing gifts."

"Come on in. I can pop a coffee pod in the machine for you."

"I was counting on that." Jeremiah grinned and kicked off his shoes. "You said you were up."

"I am." Danny gestured to himself. "Do you see me in bed?"

"Nah. But I do recognize pajama pants when I see them."

"You didn't ask how long I'd been up." Danny headed back toward the kitchen. Jeremiah would follow if he wanted coffee, and that was what Danny wanted more than anything right now. "Why are you out and about this early?"

"It's after ten, man." Jeremiah dropped the bakery box on the kitchen table and moved toward the cupboard where Danny kept his mugs.

Danny got his coffee and dumped in sugar. "It's a holiday."

"True. But handymen know no holidays. In fact, I'd say it's better than even odds that I end up fixing at least three garbage disposals today. I've already hit my mom's. She never listens when I tell her not to put the potato peels down the thing." Jeremiah popped a pod into the machine and pressed the start button.

Danny sat at the table and flipped open the box lid. He considered the varied options before plucking out a doughnut with chocolate and sprinkles on the top. He took a bite and could practically feel the sugar hit his bloodstream.

Jeremiah brought his coffee over and spun the box so he could see inside. "So."

"What?" Danny took a swig from his mug.

"You disappeared yesterday."

"I said I was going to check on Claire."

"Uh huh. Then you didn't come back." Jeremiah bit off half of his doughnut with one bite.

Weren't there limits to what had to be shared with friends? "She wanted company. We watched White Christmas."

"How is she?"

Danny scrubbed a hand over his face. "Look, man, I just woke up. What are you getting at?"

"Dee's worried. Claire wouldn't talk to her last night. Or this morning. And, frankly, Dee needs her sister right now, because this thing with their parents . . . she didn't see it coming."

"Neither did Claire." Danny drank. The caffeine needed to hurry up and kick in before he said something he shouldn't. Claire had made a few comments over the course of the evening —nothing earth shattering—but still nothing he was probably supposed to share. "She's having a hard time. It's shaken her. More, I think, than seems reasonable."

"What's reasonable? I mean seriously, their parents are splitting up."

"No, I get that. But they're adults. Neither of them lives at home. They have their own lives. How's Duncan doing?"

"No idea. He and Anna disappeared right around the same time you did yesterday and they haven't left the cottage yet today. Or at least, not that I've seen. And I did check for their cars before heading out."

Danny nodded. Sexist though it might be, he didn't imagine Duncan was thrown quite as badly as his sisters. Or, if he was, he was unlikely to show it. But he could still be there—be the rock —for his sisters. "I think Claire will be okay. In time. She had a week's head start on the announcement, but I don't think it helped with her processing."

"She what?" Jeremiah set his mug down on the table with a bang. "Why wouldn't she say something?"

Oh man. Danny winced. He'd really put his foot in it now. "You can't say anything to Deidre about that."

"What? No way. Dee—"

"Doesn't need to know." Danny held up a hand. "Hear me out."

Jeremiah blew out a breath. "Make it good."

"Dee's what, seven months pregnant?"

"Close enough. What does that have to do with anything?"

"I would imagine Claire didn't want to say something that would stress Deidre out. Plus, she didn't know they were going to lawyers and signing papers. She just knew that they were screaming and slamming doors. Would you have said something if you didn't have all the information?"

"Yes."

Danny frowned. "Seriously?"

"Yes. Because then my siblings could have come with me to confront my parents before they did anything irreversible."

That made a kind of sense. Still, Danny felt the need to defend Claire. "They haven't done anything irreversible yet. So . . . that could still happen. Not saying something sooner didn't preclude any sort of action."

"What are you talking about? They've filed papers." Jeremiah reached for another doughnut.

To be fair, Danny had thought the same thing until Claire explained what she'd found when she looked things up online before her nap. "It's not the same as a divorce. If, after six months, they don't do anything, they stay married. That document isn't anything more than an agreement on how their property would be divided if they file after the waiting period."

"You're sure about that?"

Danny nodded.

Jeremiah dug his phone out of his pocket.

"What are you doing?"

"Texting Deidre to let her know that. It's good information. Doesn't change the fact that Claire should have told us—if only so she had someone to share her grief."

"That part I can't argue with, but I wasn't going to say anything to her. And I don't think anyone should. Why kick her when she's down?" Danny considered a moment before adding, "She wasn't in a great place before she found out about this. Something's off with her."

Jeremiah drained his coffee and frowned at Danny. "Are you really this dense? Matt said you overheard her at church. You know she's been half in love with you for basically the last two years. What do you think is off?"

"What does one thing have to do with the other? How is this suddenly my fault?"

"Do you know why she was up in DC last week?"

"Not really. I figured she went up to see her parents."

"No. She went up for a job interview."

"An interv—but she has a job. Here. Running Peacock Hill." Why would Claire be thinking of leaving what had to be a dream position? She could work the hours she wanted. Deidre gave her total control over decisions. And Peacock Hill was turning into an amazing event destination. The Founder's Ball choosing them for this year's gala was proof of that. And hadn't he heard someone say something about them thinking of making it a permanent choice? "I'm confused."

"You've spent the last two years flirting with everything female on two legs, Danny. For a while, she'd convinced herself it was because you just weren't willing to be in a committed relationship. So she was cool with it—she didn't want to be one of your one and dones. Then you went out with Casey."

"For a long time."

Jeremiah nodded. "And Claire had no choice but to realize that it wasn't that you didn't want to be in a long term relationship. You just didn't want to be in one with her."

"But I didn't know that was even an option!" Danny threw his hands in the air. Was he supposed to be a mind reader now? The woman didn't throw herself at him. She was just friendly. Sure, they'd hung out and flirted harmlessly, but that's all that it had been. At least, that's all that it had seemed like it was supposed to be. "I didn't see it."

"Yeah, well, everyone else did."

"Why didn't you say something?"

"Don't even start, man. We did. You didn't hear." Jeremiah shook his head. "Anyway, I guess she decided she didn't want to wait around any longer. I don't think it's all about you—Deidre got the vibe that there's something else at play in addition—but she's looking around and Jamie Fisher is looking to snap her up."

The dude from the ball. And the restaurant. That figured. She couldn't be serious about that other guy though. Not the way she'd kissed Danny last night.

"So?"

Danny pulled his mind back from memories of their time on the couch and shot Jeremiah a confused look.

"Are you finally going to admit you like her? Maybe do something about it? Convince her to stay here?"

"Yes. Yes. And I'll try."

Jeremiah offered a sharp nod. "Do that."

～

"Do you think you have enough Christmas trees?" Danny eyed the stack of tied up evergreens on the front porch of Peacock Hill. "What are there, eight?"

"Ten." Claire shook her head and pointed to the smaller pile of trees in the driveway. "Deidre got carried away. Jeremiah's convinced it's nesting. Their apartment is set and ready for the baby, so she's turning her eye to Christmas decorations. Honestly? I'm pleased she made it until after Thanksgiving. She's been after me to start since Halloween. I held her off because of the ball."

"I was about to ask." Danny blew out a breath. "Tell me where to take them."

"You're going to help?"

He nodded, his insides warming at the look of hopeful relief on her face. "Jeremiah said it was all hands on deck. I have hands."

"Thank you thank you thank you!" Claire threw her arms around him and gave him a quick squeeze before blushing red and stepping away. She cleared her throat. "Matt and Azure had Dee and Jer over after church. They won't be back for a bit and I wasn't sure—"

"Why didn't you go?"

She shrugged. "I get tired of being fifth wheel. They invited me. They invited Duncan and Anna, too, but Anna's not feeling well and wanted a nap."

"Is she okay?"

Claire glanced over her shoulder before stepping closer. "Between you and me? I think she's pregnant. They haven't said anything, but that's my guess."

"Oh, wow. That's—" Danny broke off at the rumble of tires on the gravel driveway and turned to eye the car heading toward the mansion. It was sort of familiar, but it didn't belong to anyone who was here regularly. "Who's that, do you think?"

Claire shaded her eyes then grinned. "I think it's Sean."

Sean. Danny searched his memory and finally came up with a face. "The wedding planner guy?"

"Yeah. Oh, he'll be a big help. I didn't know he was coming."

Danny could be a big help. What was the guy doing here unannounced? Not that the gang at Peacock Hill stood on any sort of ceremony. Danny was here technically uninvited more often than not. Didn't mean he had to love it when other people did it. "Do you have any weddings scheduled?"

"Not until New Year's Eve. Larissa's here, too. We might just get these all done today. She has a good eye." Claire hurried down the steps and met the car as it came to a stop behind Danny's.

Danny followed more slowly behind Claire. If the guy brought someone along, it probably meant he wasn't after Claire. He was just reaching the bottom of the stairs when Claire squealed and started jumping up and down, holding on to Larissa's hand.

"Oh my gosh! Congratulations! It's a gorgeous ring. Danny," Claire gestured for him to come closer, "Look. Isn't it gorgeous?"

Danny glanced down at the diamonds sparkling in a circle on Larissa's left hand and smiled. "Definitely. Congrats."

"He proposed on Thanksgiving, right after the meal." Larissa shot Sean a loving look. "It was sweet."

"I was going for romantic, but I'll take sweet." Sean grinned. "Anyway, we wanted to let everyone here know. You're all sort of responsible for us being together. Where is everyone?"

"They'll be here in a couple of hours. Want to help set up Christmas trees while you wait?" Claire nodded to the stacks of festivity waiting to happen.

Sean laughed. "Why not? Where do they go?"

"The tree stands are in position. Basically any room with windows on the main floor. Two on the big landing on either side of the stained glass window. Duncan and Anna are taking one to the cottage and then Deidre and I each get one in our apartments in the basement."

"Wow." Larissa laughed. "Do you have enough ornaments?"

"Deidre went crazy, so probably. I think she also went simple though, just different colored balls. But I have instructions, because she has themes and patterns in mind." Claire nodded. "Oh, you heard me."

Sean glanced at Danny. "How about you and I do the manual labor and leave the rest to the women."

"That sounds about right to me. I think maybe pregnancy has cost Deidre her mind." Danny started back up the front steps. Grunting with the effort, he hefted up a tree. "Could you get the door?"

"Sure. Then you want me to grab an end? I think we'll do better working together."

Might as well. Sean was probably right. The tree was heavy. And while he probably could get it in the stand on his own, why risk it when there was someone else who could help? Even if he'd rather that someone was Claire.

Sean and Danny muscled the tree into the house and up the stairs to the landing. Danny balanced the tree while Sean opened the screws in the tree stand. When it was placed, straight, and the stand was tight enough that it wouldn't tip, the both stood back to admire.

"One down. How many more to go?"

Danny chuckled. "I guess you didn't think you'd get put to work when you decided to come down."

"I don't mind. But no." Sean started down the stairs. "So just you and Claire, huh?"

There was more to the question hanging heavily in the air. Had everyone known about Claire's crush? Well, everyone but him. Danny lifted a shoulder. One of the things he wanted to talk to her about today was where they stood. But the trees had derailed that portion of the conversation. Maybe he could get her alone at dinner. Or after. Because he really wanted to know. "Yeah. Or at least, I think so."

"About time." Sean clapped him on the shoulder and bent to lift the bottom of another tree from the porch. "You have a good Thanksgiving here? Deidre invited us, but since I had plans of my own, and I think my mother might have had a heart attack if we hadn't gone to her house, we couldn't make it work."

Danny started up the steps to the side of the landing opposite the first tree. "It was . . . memorable. I'm going with that."

"There's a story there." Sean set his end of the tree down and worked on the stand for a moment before giving Danny a nod.

As Danny set the trunk in the stand, he tried to figure out how much to say. Deidre considered nearly everyone family. She opened her home and her heart without a moment's hesitation. But Claire and Duncan were more private. Would they want Sean to know about their parents? Maybe they wouldn't care, but was it his place to make that decision? "Mr. and Mrs. McIntyre were down. It wasn't a smooth visit."

Claire set a box down on the landing.

Larissa deposited another beside it.

"We'll start decorating here, now that you've got them set up. What wasn't smooth?" Claire tugged the lid off a box revealing smaller boxes with clear fronts displaying peacock blue and green decorative balls. "She doesn't miss a trick, does she?"

"Dee? No. She has an eye. Those will look great here by the window." Danny started back down the stairs.

"You didn't answer my question."

He winced and turned. "Sean asked about Thanksgiving. I wasn't sure how much to say."

"Oh." Everything about Claire seemed to deflate. Danny wanted nothing more than to wrap her in his arms. She turned a sad smile toward Sean. "My parents are splitting up. Unless a miracle happens in the next six months."

Sean reached out and rubbed Claire's arm. "I'm sorry."

"Me, too." Larissa grabbed Claire's hand. "It makes all these trees a little more understandable though."

Huh? Danny tried to figure out how one related to the other. Finally asking, "How?"

"I imagine Deidre's been acting like it's fine. No big deal, right?"

Claire frowned. "Kinda. We've had some good conversations in private, but mostly she acts like it's not happening."

"She's in denial and overcompensating." Larissa gestured to the trees. "I see it with my students when they're hurting. It's a defense mechanism. When a kid's heart hurts, they don't figure out why and how to fix it, they just act out. Sometimes that means I get a class clown. Sometimes it means stealing other kids' pencils and breaking them or getting into fights on the playground. In Deidre's case, it appears that because one area of her life is falling apart, she's going to do everything she can to make the rest of it bigger and brighter so she doesn't have to think about it."

"Teacher and psychologist, all wrapped in one." Danny grinned to soften the words. He wasn't poking fun, nor was he saying she was wrong, but why could someone who barely knew everyone here figure that out when he and Claire hadn't?

Larissa shrugged. "I could be wrong."

"No. I don't think you are." Claire sat on the top step and propped her chin in her hands. "That's Dee's M.O."

"You think?" Danny climbed back up and sat beside Claire. He took one of her hands and gave it a gentle squeeze. When she didn't pull away, he kissed her knuckles and let their clasped hands rest on her knee.

"Look at this place. It's one big overcompensation. Her flipping show and handyman business in DC hit the rocks—and I'm not downplaying the fact that it was because of that jerk she was seeing, but I don't think the motivation matters—and instead of retooling and regrouping, she decides to buy this dump and make it something spectacular. And she has. But I'm not sure that she's really okay with how things went before she got here." Claire rested her head briefly on Danny's shoulder before straightening. "But none of that is getting the trees decorated. And if Dee gets through the awful things in her life with big projects, I do it by marking off items on my to-do list. So let's get cracking."

Danny laughed and stood, tugging her to her feet. "Yes, ma'am."

"Right behind you, man." Sean followed Danny down the stairs and back onto the porch. "I'm glad you and Claire are figuring things out. It'll help her."

"I hope so." Now that he was looking at Claire without friendship blinders, he wanted nothing more than to have her as a permanent fixture in his life. But he couldn't shake the feeling that he was part of her plan to get through the pain of her parents' decisions, and nothing else.

11

C laire scanned the tables in the crowded bistro but didn't see Jamie. She returned her gaze to the hostess and smiled. "I don't think he's here yet. Table for two?"

"Sure." The girl—because in Claire's estimation she wasn't twenty yet, or, if she was, it was barely—looked down at the table map on her podium, made a mark, and collected two menus. "Right this way."

The tight path through the tables confirmed that this was a popular lunch spot with any sort of crowd. There were college students with their bulging backpacks who were clearly planning to stay and work after their meals were consumed. There were groups of office workers in the business casual uniform of sweaters and slacks, maybe the occasional skirt. Upper management, in their thinly pinstriped suits and red power ties were dotted throughout. And there were moms in jeans and long-sleeved T-shirts, hair up in messy buns and frazzled glances to verify the time before, Claire imagined, they had to hurry off to collect their offspring.

"Your server will be right with you." The hostess dropped the menus on the table and disappeared back through the crowd to the front of the restaurant.

Claire flipped open the menu and studied the offerings. Her only time constraint was getting back from Charlottesville in time to help Matt with youth group. So if Jamie was late, well, later than he already was, it was fine.

Nerves jumped in her stomach. He had to be bringing her a job offer. They could have emailed it. The woman in HR had all but said that was how it would be handled. But Jamie had taken a personal interest—both in Claire's career and in Claire herself.

She wasn't sure what to do about either of them.

Danny . . . kissing Danny . . . wow. And it hadn't been just the one time in the kitchen. No, he'd snuggled in with her on the couch and put up with her singing along with Bing Crosby and Danny Kaye, and he'd kissed her in the movie's slow spots.

She'd never realized just how many slow spots that movie had.

Heat seeped into her cheeks, and she reached for the glass of water a server had deposited along with a promise to be right back while he was frantically running between tables.

"Sorry I'm late." Jamie wore the upper management uniform well, though his suit was charcoal gray instead of black and his tie was a dizzying swirl of color. He slid into the seat across from Claire and set a leather portfolio on the table. "It's good to see you."

"Thanks. I appreciate you meeting halfway."

"I'll spoil it and say I was in Charlottesville anyway. We have a satellite office here. It's small, but we've got some proposals on tap that might end up expanding operations. We should hear on those this month and, since I'm feeling optimistic, I've been looking at new office space that would accommodate some growth." Jamie reached across the table and touched her hand. "How are you?"

He knew about her parents. She'd told him the whole thing when she'd been in DC. His concern was visible. "I'm okay. Still processing, I guess. They told everyone at Thanksgiving. I guess I wish they hadn't chosen a holiday for that, but we were all together so it probably makes sense in their convoluted world."

"I'm sorry."

Claire shook her head. "Don't be. I'm sorry. I . . . let's talk about something else. How was your Thanksgiving? Big family gathering?"

Jamie laughed. "Oh, yeah. Mom doesn't do small holidays. Vanessa and Topher were there, so of course ninety percent of the conversation was wedding related. Dad and I escaped to watch football as soon as we could, even though neither of us are diehard fans. But it was better than rose petal colors and Mom's continued attempts to get Topher to legally change his name to Christopher."

Claire laughed. "She isn't."

"Oh. She is. Poor guy. He has no idea what he's in for." Jamie shook his head, but he smiled.

Claire figured Topher probably had a decent handle on things. And, knowing Topher from the weddings he'd worked at Peacock Hill, he'd bring Mrs. Fisher around and probably convince her it'd been her idea for him to be called that in the first place. "When's the wedding?"

"They don't have a date yet. They're still arguing—pardon me, discussing—venues. Mom wants to rent the National Cathedral."

Claire laughed again. "No way."

"Oh yeah. I guess she has a frenemy whose daughter was married there two years ago. If there was a way to top it, Mom would be looking for that, but really, how do you top the cathedral?"

"A frenemy? Really? I thought those were for seventeen-year-old stars of reality TV dramas."

"And, apparently, rich old women with nothing better to do. But now, since it made you laugh, I'm kind of glad Mom has one. For a moment, all the sad lurking in your eyes disappeared."

"Jamie . . ."

The server reappeared to take their order, cutting Claire off. Which was probably a good thing. She wasn't completely sure what she was going to say—but something in the way Jamie looked at her needed to be addressed.

How? Well, that was the question, wasn't it?

When the server disappeared with their menus and orders, Jamie slid his portfolio in front of him and flipped it open. "How about we get business out of the way, then we can enjoy our lunch."

"Okay." A change in subject seemed like just the thing. She reached for the presentation folder he offered.

"The top page is your offer letter. It has the basics—salary, title, a brief description of your duties. I don't think there are any surprises in there, but if you have questions I can answer them. The rest is the usual new hire paperwork for medical and dental, retirement plans, blah blah blah." He flicked his fingers at her. "Go ahead and open it. Do you want me to leave for a minute?"

"No, you don't have to do that." Claire smiled and opened the folder. She skimmed the letter until she got to the position and salary. Her mouth went dry and she glanced up at Jamie. "This isn't—that's not—I didn't interview for this."

"You did and you didn't."

Claire frowned. "Explain. Please?"

"The position you interviewed for when you came up is open. And if it's really what you want, we can talk about that. But, Claire, you have to know you can do more than that.

Everyone you talked to agrees that you'd be well suited for the position in the letter. You didn't think it odd that you spoke to so many people in upper management?"

She hunched her shoulders. Sure, it had been a little weird, but how was she supposed to know what was usual? "I've never interviewed—or worked—at a big company. You know that."

"Right. I forgot."

She tipped her head to the side and studied him. It was possible he'd forgotten. But it seemed unlikely. Did it matter?

Jamie's smile was the same one she'd seen her brother use as a little kid when he was trying to charm his way out of trouble. "I'm sorry?"

Darn it. At some point, shouldn't boyish charm stop being a thing? "Yeah, okay."

He grinned. "Good. I really want you to come work for me, Claire. And with this job, we'd interact a lot. It'd be a great chance for us to see how things develop. On a business level. And a more personal one."

Claire bit her lip. The little she'd read of the job duties were a dream. And, on the one hand, being around Jamie and working with him would help them develop a relationship. On the flip side, wasn't one of the primary rules of the corporate world that business and pleasure didn't mix? If she took the job at the same time as they started exploring a more personal relationship, what would people think? And say?

"I'm going to need some time to think about it."

"WHAT'S THIS, MISS CLAIRE?" One of the youth held out the portfolio holding her job offer and the company information Jamie had given her. She'd had only enough time to shove it into her bag and hit the road when she and Jamie had finally parted ways. As it was, she'd missed the very beginning of youth group.

Her cheeks heated and she grabbed for the folder. "Just . . . information. Did you find a pen?"

The girl nodded, frowning. "Are you leaving?"

"Why would you ask that?" Claire hated the defensiveness that had crept into her voice, but honestly, what had she been doing looking inside it? Grab a pen, sure. Paw through her belongings? That had not been on offer.

"The pen was hooked to the edge. I kind of saw some words." The girl's eyes glistened. "I don't want you to go."

Sighing, Claire hooked her arm around the girl's shoulders. "I'm just thinking about it. It's so up in the air right now, it might as well be a satellite."

"Those are in orbit—in space. There's no air there."

In spite of herself, Claire laughed. "Even better. It's nebulous, okay? Don't mention it to anyone, though."

"Why not?"

"Because it's so uncertain. I don't want to get anyone's hopes up. Or down." She sure didn't want word getting back to Deidre. Claire had, so far, successfully avoided getting into the details of the interview in DC before Thanksgiving. Her parents and their dumb news had sidetracked her brother and sister quite nicely. But she didn't want anything drawing their attention back to that overdue conversation. The fact that Jamie had given her time to think things over was perfect. Maybe she could draw it out until February. After Deidre gave birth. Then, at least, Claire would know she hadn't been responsible for her sister going into labor.

"Can I pray that God keeps you here?"

"Of course you can. But I guess I'd rather you pray that I know God's will and do it."

The girl considered before nodding. "Okay. But I don't see

how it could be God's will that you leave. We need you here. And Mr. Danny needs you in his life. If you take a job in DC, that's not going to happen."

How much had the girl read? "Mr. Danny and I are friends, hon, nothing more."

Now she laughed. "I guess grownups don't know any better than teenagers. Have you ever watched him watch you?"

By definition, the answer to that had to be no. How would she watch him watch her? As soon as he saw her looking, he'd look away. Or smile and do something goofy. "No. How does he watch me?"

"There's this old movie my mom likes and she watches it constantly after Christmas."

"Oh? Which one?" Following the thought trains of teenagers often sent her for a loop, but, more often than not, they got back to the point they were trying to make if she hung in there.

"*While You Were Sleeping*. Have you seen it?" The girl fixed Claire with a hopeful gaze.

Old movie? It wasn't that old, was it? "Sure. I love that one, too."

The girl barely stopped her eyes from rolling. "Figures. Anyway, you know the scene where the creepy guy brings the girl a big weird flower arrangement?"

Claire thought for a moment. "Yeah, I think so. It's a big wreath, right?"

The girl grinned. "Yeah. And creepy guy says he sees how Lucy looks at the other guy like she just saw her first Trans Am? I had to Google what that was, and it's a seriously ugly car, but I guess it used to be hot. And anyway, that's how Mr. Danny looks at you. Except maybe a nicer car, 'cause you're really pretty."

"Thanks." What else was there to say? Somewhere in there, the girl had paid her a compliment. She didn't necessarily believe that Danny looked at her anything like that, though.

Certainly he hadn't before they'd kissed. He'd been too hung up on all his various girlfriends. Hadn't he? Since the kiss . . . es . . . kisses, because they'd spent a lot of time on her couch—and she'd ended the evening glad that she'd seen White Christmas more times than she could count, because they'd missed a lot of it—they'd really only hung out when it was tree day. He'd been back to his usual friendly self for that. No real flirting.

Certainly no kisses.

And all that had left her wondering if she'd ended up as one of his meaningless conquests after all.

12

Danny tossed his pencil onto his desk and pushed back, shooting the chair across the hardwood floor of his home office. It was Friday, night and he was working. It wasn't even work he needed to do, he was just doing it because he had nothing else to do. It might make his client happy, but it sure didn't please him.

Everyone at Peacock Hill was buttoned in for the night. Couple time. He frowned. He should be happy for them. Encouraging it, in fact. After all, married couples needed to spend time together. Alone. Without friends and siblings. There was nothing wrong with them deciding no movie night. Just maybe a little more advance notice would be nicer next time. So he could . . . what? Line up a date? Not happening.

He sighed and rolled back to the desk.

Not unless he could convince Claire to go out with him.

Claire.

She was probably hanging around in her little basement apartment with nothing to do, too.

Unless she had a date?

His gut clenched.

It was a possibility though. It wasn't like he had a claim on her. They'd made no declarations. They hadn't even really talked about the after-Thanksgiving movie. That's what he was calling it. Saying kissing—even in his head—brought it all back too clearly. That was not the recipe for restful nights.

So what? Call her? Text her? Text. Something casual. Hey girl, what's up?

No. That was creepy. Trying too hard. And like one of those strange Internet memes that old women fawned over.

He grabbed his phone and flipped open a message. Too much thinking.

Hey. How's your Friday?

Danny hit send. It wasn't much better than first thought, but at least it was more like his voice. This was crazy. She was probably watching a movie. Or sleeping. Or out. Or—his phone buzzed.

Eh. Can't settle on a movie so I'm watching Hallmark Christmas cheese.

He laughed.

I thought you'd totally go for that. Why cheese?

His phone rang.

"Too much to type. And you're not wrong. Normally I'd go for every one of the Christmas movies they put on. But this year? I don't know, it's all so unrealistic. I mean you have these people and they fall in love and the movie ends like it's going to last forever, but it won't. Down the road twenty, thirty years? One of them will decide it's all too much effort and that'll be that."

Danny winced. Her parents. "It doesn't have to be like that."

"I know that. I do. But who's to say it won't? I mean seriously, your parents split up. Mine are splitting up. Love is a crock."

His heart broke at the pain in her voice. "I don't have any words that can make it better. I wish I did."

"No. It's okay. I'm just . . . my brother and sister ditch me, right, so they can spend time with their spouses. Why? What's the point? I'm their sister. I'm not going to walk out of their life. Can they say the same for the person they married?"

"What's the alternative? Give up on love completely? Never date? Never marry? Isn't it better to believe that God can keep a marriage together if both parties are willing to let Him?"

There was silence, then Claire snorted. "Listen to you, Mr. Spiritual now, are we? What happened to love 'em and leave 'em Danny? Or is that only when it comes to me?"

"What do you mean?" He rubbed his breastbone, trying to soothe the sudden burning.

"Were you figuring we'd just ignore it forever? I can do that. But you don't get to tell me love is worth chasing when we spend an evening on my couch with our lips locked and then you act like nothing happened."

"I act like nothing happened? That, my dear, was you. I was following your lead."

"Please. We set up how many trees? And you never once—"

"What was I supposed to do in front of Sean and Larissa? And then the rest of the gang when they showed up? Did you want me to put my arm around you? Kiss you under the mistletoe? Because I would have happily done all of that, but I didn't because I thought you'd be angry and embarrassed if I did."

"Oh sure. That's convenient." Claire huffed out a breath. "Fine. What about since then?"

"When? I haven't seen you all week, except briefly across the room at youth group when you were talking to Sissy. I didn't want to interrupt. By the time you were finished, I was helping Junior, whose mother just found out her breast cancer is back for the third time."

"Oh no. I hadn't heard that." She sighed. "I feel stupid."

"Don't. Love does strange things to our brains." Danny bit his lip. Maybe he should have taken the time to think of a better word, but love had popped out. And it felt right.

"Danny. I—"

"I'm not saying I love you, Claire. I'm not asking you to say you love me."

"Then what are you saying?"

"I'm saying I want to have the right to kiss you again. And I don't want anyone else to have that right. As high school as it sounds, I want you to be my girlfriend, Claire." There. It was out in the open. And it was like someone had pulled a huge weight off his chest.

Claire snickered. "Sorry." She snorted and it turned into a full-blown laugh.

Wasn't that just great? He laid his heart at her feet and she had paroxysms of laughter. He waited for her mirth to subside. "Or not."

"Oh no. No, no, no. You don't get to take that back."

"I don't know. I think maybe I do when it's met with hilarity."

"I'm sorry. It's just funny."

"So I gathered. Mind telling me why?"

"Two years. You've had two years to get to this point and when you finally do, there's someone else."

Someone else. He swallowed. "Jamie. He moves fast."

"No. I mean, yeah, Jamie, but there's nothing official." The unspoken "yet" hung in the air. "But I got this amazing job offer and it'd mean moving to DC and I'd be at his company and . . ."

"I get it." He was too late. Figured. But he could be a friend. He was good at that. "Well, congratulations."

"Hey, hold up."

"What?"

"Danny."

He groaned under his breath. He wasn't going to ask "what" again. "Claire."

"You just asked me to be your girlfriend."

"I know. And you laughed at me and told me I was too late. It's all right. Really. Like I said, I get it. And the job in DC is probably amazing and if that's where God is leading you, then you should totally go. I hope we can still be friends though." He winced. Was that as bad as "it's not you, it's me?" Of course, he wasn't breaking up with her. She'd dumped him. Or turned him down. It wasn't really a dumping when there'd been no relationship to start with, right?

"I don't—it's not that straightforward."

He frowned. So they couldn't even be friends? That would be awkward, but not insurmountable. The last six months or so had been strained. It'd probably go back to that. Not ideal, but at least now, if the guys tried to give him grief about it, he could point out that she'd been the one to end things before they'd had a chance to start. That had to count for something. "Okay. Look, I'm tired. It's been a long week. I'm gonna go. Maybe I'll see you around this weekend. Night, Claire."

She might have been saying something as he ended the call, but he didn't care. His heart could only take so much. All the weight he'd felt lift when he finally got the words out settled right back on his chest. And it was heavier.

DANNY RUBBED a hand over the stubble on his chin. He should shave. Except it was Saturday. And it was unlikely he was going to be kissing anyone any time soon. So really. Why bother?

He dragged on jeans and a sweatshirt. Jeremiah had texted at seven asking if Danny had time to help with a project at Peacock Hill today. Why the guy couldn't have waited until a decent hour was unknown, but now that he was up, Danny didn't have anything better to do.

He shoved his feet into sneakers, grabbed a jacket just in case, and headed for the car. He'd swing by the diner and get a box of doughnuts. There were usually fresh doughnuts on Saturday and it was early enough that he ought to be able to snag some for the guys.

The guys. Would the ladies be joining them? Jeremiah hadn't said. Depending on the project, Deidre was probably out. Unless it was a baby-related project, in which case she'd be there supervising with a vengeance. That woman . . . she knew what she wanted and would boss people around until it was just right. It's probably what made her so great at her job, but he was glad she wasn't his wife.

Despite being Deidre's sister, Claire was much more laid back. Even though Claire's profession was basically organizing events and telling people what to do.

And he shouldn't be thinking about Claire. He was too late. He'd lost the battle to Jamie before he'd even realized he wanted to be in the game.

The drive through his old, forested neighborhood soothed. Not many people were out at half past seven on a Saturday morning. Especially not at the start of December when, even if the projected high was fifty-two degrees, there was still a thick frost on the ground and the numbers on his dash glowed in the upper thirties. By the time he got home, he expected that more of the houses would have strung lights and hung wreaths in preparation for Christmas, which was right around the corner.

He needed to do his shopping.

After Thanksgiving, he'd entertained the briefest fantasy of offering Claire a ring. It had been out there even before she'd made it clear that their lip lock was a one-time thing. Six weeks of dating wasn't really enough before an engagement. Not even after a two-year friendship. At least that was what he'd told himself.

Now?

Well, now it was good he'd seen reason. He'd been awfully close to buying something he'd found on the website of a Charlottesville jeweler. The shop wasn't far from his office—it'd be an easy enough stop to make on his way to or from work on any given day.

Danny meandered down Main, snagging a parking spot an easy walk to the diner. If there was going to be a crowd anywhere on a Saturday morning, the diner was the place to find it. He tossed greetings to the older men and couples he knew—one of the perks of small town life—while he waited for the doughnuts to get boxed up. With a wave, he took the box and jogged back to his car.

It didn't take long to get out of town and wind up the mountain to Peacock Hill. Swinging around the curve in the driveway he caught his first glimpse of the mansion. The view never failed to cause a hitch in his breath. It was so beautiful. Today, though, it was mixed with something else. He desperately wanted to see Claire.

He just as desperately hoped she wasn't around.

With a sigh, he parked behind Azure Patterson's vintage truck. If the truck was here, that meant Matt, at least, had brought his wife. Azure didn't tend to let anyone else drive her old Studebaker. Maybe the women would go off on their own.

His heart wasn't going to be able to handle an all-hands gathering where he and Claire were the only singles and, therefore, a de facto couple.

Why hadn't he appreciated it when he had the chance to do something about it?

Danny grabbed the bakery box and jogged up the steps to the front door. A cursory knock and he pushed the door open, calling out, "Hello?"

"Hey man. Dining room."

That was Jeremiah's voice. There were other people talking —he could almost pick out the voices. Not all of them were men, dang it.

He fixed a smile in place and sauntered around the corner to the dining room. Enormous bowls of popcorn sat on the table beside smaller, but still huge, bowls of something round and red. Cranberries? "We're not stringing popcorn. You didn't wake me up at seven on a Saturday to string popcorn, right?"

"Not to worry. The men are doing something appropriately manly." Deidre glanced up, rubbing her pregnant belly. "There's a ton of deadfall that needs clearing out near the fire pit. It'd make good material for fires, and we have a couple of groups booked for an outdoor evening of carols and s'mores, so it'd be great to have the wood prepped and ready."

Danny nodded and slid the box down the table toward Deidre. "In that case, I'll share the doughnuts."

"Oh. You really shouldn't have." Deidre eyed the box and pressed her lips together. "I shouldn't."

"Sure you should, you're eating for two." Jeremiah flipped open the box and drew out a chocolate covered treat. "Mmm. The diner? No one beats diner doughnuts. Thanks, man."

Deidre chewed her lip for a moment before plucking out a treat of her own. Then she closed the lid and shoved the box away from her. "Eat them. Or I will."

Danny chuckled and reached for his own. "I saw Azure's truck. Is Matt helping with the wood?"

Jeremiah nodded. "They went down to talk to Claire. Duncan's coming too, but he'll meet us at the fire pit. Anna's not feeling well."

Danny watched Jeremiah and Deidre exchange a look. He was missing something, obviously, but he wasn't going to ask. If someone wanted him to know, they'd tell him. "Okay. So we're waiting for Matt?"

"Waiting. Like you've been here more than five minutes." Matt stamped into the room and shook his head. "You weren't here, that's why we went down to see Claire. She said she'd be up in thirty, by the way."

Deidre frowned. "She say why?"

"Didn't ask. I figured it was Saturday, so no big. Do I smell doughnuts?" Matt's gaze locked onto the bakery box and he grinned. "Nice. You're forgiven for being late."

Azure jabbed her elbow into Matt's side.

"Ow. What was that for?" Matt took two doughnuts and pushed the box toward his wife.

"You can be so clueless sometimes," Azure muttered under her breath before looking at Danny. "How are you?"

He probably wasn't supposed to have heard the mutter, so he ignored it. It wasn't a guarantee that she was talking about him and Claire, though it seemed fairly obvious. Danny shrugged. "I'm fine. It's early—still waking up."

Azure offered a sympathetic nod. "Thanks for the doughnuts."

"Which you're not eating." Danny pointed at her.

"Mornings aren't my best time right now either." Azure glanced at Matt. He gave a tiny nod and rested his hand on her shoulder. "I'm pregnant."

Deidre squealed and levered herself out of her seat. "That's so exciting!"

"Yeah, congrats." Danny tucked his hands in his pockets. It was awkward, but what was he supposed to do? Sure, if they wanted kids, then that was great. They got married at Labor Day so that was what, three months ago? It seemed fast, just like Deidre and Jeremiah—though they'd made it closer to four months. And it was none of his business. "Guess there's a regular old baby boom going on around here."

A tiny squeak came from around the corner, then pounding footsteps and a slammed door.

Danny winced. "What did I say?"

"I don't—who was it?" Matt leaned back so he could peer around the doorway into the foyer. "I don't know. Empty now."

"It was Anna." Deidre sighed and returned her seat. Her eyes were shiny. "She must have miscarried again. It stinks that she heard you that way, but the reality is, new marriages of young people are bound to result in babies. I get that she's upset, but are we not supposed to celebrate? With all the other insanity happening in our family right now, I'm not supposed to be excited about my baby anymore because she's struggling?"

"That's not what she meant, hon." Jeremiah rubbed Deidre's shoulders.

"Felt like it. But whatever. You guys go do manly things. We'll sit in here and string cranberries and popcorn, and if Claire and Anna deign to join us, then great. If not, then I guess it's up to me and Azure to make things festive."

Make things festive? The place was already swimming in decorated trees, wreaths, mistletoe, and garlands. In fact, if Danny didn't know better, he'd assume Deidre was planning to turn the mansion into a Christmas store.

"Dee." The censure in Jeremiah's voice made Danny want to hunch his shoulders.

"All right. Fine." A pout formed on Deidre's lips and she huffed out a breath. "I'll heave my bulky self over there and see what I can do."

"Maybe you should send Claire." The words were out before Danny could stop them.

Deidre shot daggers at him. "Oh yeah? Why's that?"

"You're . . ." Danny gestured to her belly. He might be a clueless man, but even he could figure out that someone practically bursting with a baby wasn't the best choice to console someone who'd just lost hers. Not when there were other options.

"Right. Of course."

"I can go." Azure started to stand.

Danny shook his head. "She heard you. I really think Claire—"

"Fine. You go tell her. The rest of you men, go chop logs. Danny knows where the fire pit is. He can meet you up there after he sends Claire on her mission of mercy."

Danny opened his mouth but found no words. He snapped it shut. He could ask someone else to do it, but that would open up the floor for questions. That was a bad plan. Was it worse than being face to face with Claire?

There was only one way to find out.

13

Claire scowled at the tap on her door. Hadn't she told Matt and Azure she'd be up in thirty? They couldn't even pass on a simple message? Thirty minutes should have been enough time for Danny to come, meet up with the guys, and leave. Then she wouldn't have to see him. If she was lucky, she could avoid seeing him . . . there was no way to make it as long as it was going to take for her to move to DC. But she could at least put off the inevitable.

Carrying her coffee with her, she padded to the door and opened it, jerking slightly when her gaze landed on Danny. "Danny."

"Hi. There's kind of an emergency. Deidre needs you to go talk to Anna." He turned and started to walk down the hallway.

"Wait. What? Why? Get back here and talk sense, please."

He stopped, turned, and crossed his arms. "Azure's expecting. Anna overheard. She apparently has been having miscarriages. Or has at least had one. I don't know. Regardless, the consensus is that you need to go talk to Anna."

"Because I'm not pregnant. Got it." Claire shook her head. What a mess. Poor Anna. "Before I do that—why are you mad?"

His eyebrows shot up. "Really, Claire?"

"Yes, really. Maybe I'm stupid, but I don't see why you should be mad."

"You're not stupid. Why do you do that?" He took a step forward and hooked his thumbs in his pockets. "And I think it's okay for me to be mad when I realize that the person I've wanted all along is standing right in front of me and I'm too late. And even though you're the one who said we couldn't at least try and still be friends, I'm not mad at you. I'm mad at me."

"Oh." Wait, when had she said they couldn't be friends? On the phone last night? "I never said that, though."

"You did. I said I hoped we could still hang out. You said it wasn't that straightforward. I get it. I've never been great at the 'let's be friends' thing anyway. But I think I would have done okay with you." He shrugged. "Anyway. Go talk to Anna. The guys are waiting for me at the fire pit. I'll see you around."

"Danny, wait."

He sighed and turned, an expectant look on his face.

What were the words? She was usually pretty good with them, but today they seemed to get caught somewhere under her breastbone. She didn't want to lose him—not as a friend. Not as the potential for more. Not after Thanksgiving.

Thanksgiving.

She closed the distance between them and, before she could change her mind, pressed her lips to his.

His arms slid around her, and he pulled her close. Claire cupped his face in with one hand, her other hand braced on his chest. Soon—too soon for her liking—Danny stepped back and locked his gaze with hers.

"What was that? What about you and Jamie?"

She stepped forward so their bodies touched. "There isn't a me and Jamie. There's just the possibility of it. He'd like it to happen. I was willing to give it a try on the off chance it would help me get over you."

"Get over . . .?"

"I love you, Danny Kent."

He blinked. Then grinned. "Really?"

Her stomach knotted. Did he not feel the same? Wasn't the appropriate response to say he loved her, too? She gave a slight nod.

Danny's arms slid around her again and he held her close. "I love you, Claire McIntyre. I think maybe I have for the last two years. You're really not seeing Jamie?"

Seeing him? They'd been having some business conversations, and okay, sure, he'd been clear about wanting more, but they hadn't made any declarations. "I'm not."

"So if I asked you to be my girlfriend—exclusively—again today, you wouldn't just laugh at me?"

"I didn't—" She stopped herself and took a breath. The vulnerability in his eyes wasn't what she was used to seeing. Not from Danny. He was confident—cocky even. "Yes."

"Just to be clear, that's a yes to being with me?"

Claire chuckled and kissed him. "Any more questions?"

"Just one. Are you free tonight?"

"I don't know. I might have plans with my boyfriend."

"Oh? What time is he picking you up?"

"You wanna say four?"

"Four is good." He kissed her, long, slow, and deep. "You should still go talk to Anna."

Claire rested her head on Danny's shoulder, drawing comfort from the knowledge that he cared. Hopefully, God would help her find the words she needed for Anna, because she didn't have a clue.

"How'd it go today?" Claire looked over at Danny as he drove down the driveway leading away from Peacock Hill. Excitement bubbled in her chest—she was actually on a date with him!

"Good. We got almost all of the deadfall cleared, chopped, and stacked. I still think you're going to need to buy some wood if you're having as many winter bonfires as it sounds like you have scheduled, but maybe I'll be wrong."

Hmm. Deidre had mentioned that as a possibility. Maybe she should just go ahead and get a cord delivered. There were some folks at church who sold split and dried wood. It was just a matter of asking the right people. "If we bought some, would we need different storage?"

"I don't think so. Jeremiah's got a great setup for keeping it off the ground and covered. There's room for probably twice what we stacked. Why?" Danny glanced over and took her hand.

Claire laced her fingers through his. "I'll talk to Dee, but I think we'll go ahead and buy some. The worst thing we could do is run out and not notice until a group was already on the way. It's not like we don't have wood burning fireplaces throughout the house. Anna and Duncan have a big one, too. If we have wood, it'll get used."

"How's Anna?"

"She'll be all right. She's tougher than she lets on. I think this morning it was just bad timing. She'd been working up the words to tell everyone, then she walks in on Azure's announcement and it was all too much. She came and strung berries and popcorn with us and was good." Maybe it had been awkward for the first thirty minutes or so, but things had evened out. Claire knew how it felt to be the odd woman out. That had been her life over the last two years as everyone around her coupled up while she had nobody. Worse than having no one, she'd had a crush on Danny, who'd been oblivious.

As Danny maneuvered onto the highway, Claire frowned. "Where are we going?"

"Ah. Wouldn't you like to know?"

"Actually, yes." She laughed. "Did you know I hate surprises?"

"Seriously?" Danny squeezed her hand before tugging his loose to merge. "What kind of person hates surprises?"

"This kind." She touched her chest with her thumb. "So. Where are we going?"

"It being Christmastime, I thought we'd find lights. I toyed with the light show at the art park in Charlottesville, but it's smaller and doesn't open until next weekend. So, Richmond."

"Wow." She settled back in her seat. "I guess it's good I like road trips."

He laughed. "It's not that far. Think about how often Sean comes out. It's maybe what, ninety minutes? We'll have time to grab some dinner before we head over to the botanical gardens."

"Oh. I love their light displays. We used to drive down as a family to see them." Claire bit her lip. Back before her parents had lost their minds and decided to destroy their family. She turned to look out the window, blinking back tears.

"Hey. Are you all right? We can do something else. There's a neighborhood light tour, we can just drive around. I thought walking would be better—especially since it's not super cold yet —but I'm flexible. We could go see a movie. I should have asked what you wanted to do."

"No." She swiped away the tears that had trickled down her cheek. "This is good. It's a great idea. I just—my parents. I don't understand it. Deidre won't really talk about it—we talk around it. Duncan . . . now that I know what's going on with Anna I guess I understand why he's been so preoccupied. I'm hurt and I'm scared."

"Why scared?" Danny set the cruise control and reached over to take her hand again.

"Because it seems like this proves that love isn't enough. And if my parents' marriage can't last, then what hope do we have, you know?"

The hum of the tires on the pavement was a subtle undercurrent for the Christmas music Danny had playing at low volume. Strains of the Hallelujah Chorus done by Christian pop singers started up.

Was he going to answer?

As the singers reached the first chorus, Danny cleared his throat. "I understand what you're saying, I do, but one person —one couple—isn't the gold standard for anyone else's relationship. Don't give up on us before we've had a chance to start."

Us. The word warmed her and she turned to study his profile as he drove.

"Everything I've read—or heard—says that marriage is work. Hard work. Any relationship is, if it's worthwhile. But that's why God has to be at the center of everything. I forgot that when I was dating Casey—it took me a while to get back to it. But, if He's the center of the relationship and the most important aspect of each person's life, then He's going to make the work manageable. Or at least help you do it."

"Why can't He just make it easy?"

Danny snorted. "You could ask that about everything in life."

It was true. Didn't make it less of a reasonable question. Why did God let so much suffering happen in the world? "We're back to the fall, right? Adam and Eve chose to sin, so the rest of us suffer."

"Would you rather not have free will?"

"Sometimes, yeah." Claire shrugged. "It'd make things easier."

"Fair. And yet, easier isn't always better. Nothing about falling in love with you has been easy."

She laughed. "That's your own fault, mister."

"Probably. But if everything had been easy and we'd slipped into a relationship simply because everyone around us coupled up and we didn't want to be alone, it wouldn't be the same."

No, it wouldn't. There was a possibility it could have been better, but there was no way to know that one way or the other, because they'd both made choices and those choices had brought them here. Was it the same with her parents? Little choices over the course of years that ended up tearing them apart instead of gluing them together? "Do you think there's any hope for my folks?"

"There's always hope, Claire. As long as we have Jesus, we always have hope."

She nodded. It sounded a little like something she'd find on a pillow at a craft store, but it didn't make it less true. Of course, her parents had a strong faith in Jesus. Or they had. Still did? That was harder to pin down. So yes, it was true, but it was also true more in an eternal sense than in a please don't let my parents split up one. For now, she could roll with it.

Hope was never a bad idea.

CLAIRE STEPPED out of the brick building at the entrance to the Richmond botanical garden. They'd purchased their entrance tickets and two large, steaming cups of coffee and could now wander as long as they wanted. Twinkling Christmas lights glittered on every plant. She glanced at Danny and grinned. "This is amazing."

"It really is. How long do you think it takes them to set this up? They can't possibly leave it all year, can they?"

"I don't think so. But it has to be at least a month of winding and wrapping and plugging things in. Which way do you want to go first?" Claire offered the map they'd been given with their tickets and sipped her drink. It might not be super cold yet, but with the sun down, it was definitely chilly.

Danny traced a route with his finger. "What if we follow this path? It takes us around the outer path and looks like we should be able to see the majority of the displays. We'll hit the greenhouse and the train setup last."

"Sure."

He glanced at the map before looking around and pointing. "That way, I think."

Danny folded the map and shoved it in his coat pocket before taking her hand in his. "Shall we?"

They walked along the gravel and crushed shell paths, weaving through clumps of people or skirting them. It was more crowded than Claire had expected—although it was an amazing light display, so she understood why so many came. There were arched wooden bridges over trickling streams that had floating, larger than life, fish made of twinkling lights. Groupings of bushes had butterflies and birds made of light. Everywhere she looked, Christmas lights glowed in fun and fantastical shapes.

"This was a good idea." Claire paused at a crossroad and glanced in each direction. "Which way?"

Danny released her hand for a moment and retrieved the map. "Do you want to see Santa's Village? They have reindeer you can pet and feed."

"Yeah? I've never actually petted a reindeer."

"Santa's Village it is." He took her hand again as they walked.

There were more families heading this direction, which made sense. What kid wouldn't want to see Santa and his reindeer? Even though her parents had never pushed the Santa thing, it was such an ingrained part of Christmas decorations she'd always enjoyed a chance to sit on his lap and make a wish.

"Claire? Is that you?"

She stopped and turned, clinging to Danny's hand. "Jamie?"

"It is you. I told Vanessa I saw you." Jamie glanced at his sister and her fiancé who stood beside him. "Didn't I tell you I saw Claire?"

"You did." Vanessa smiled. "It's good to see you. This is Danny, right?"

Claire licked her lips. "Right. Danny, you know Vanessa, right? She's done a lot of flowers for events at the Hill. And Topher? He does cakes."

"I remember Topher's cakes." Danny's smile was closer to a grimace. "And Jamie, was it?"

Jamie stuck out his hand. "James Fisher. I don't believe we've met?"

"Maybe at the ball?" Claire tugged her hand free from Danny's as nerves and dread mixed in her stomach. "I think maybe everyone met at the ball. Congratulations, by the way, Vanessa. Not only on the event, but your engagement."

Vanessa grinned. "Thanks. But you did so much more on the event, I should be congratulating you. In fact . . . don't let on that you had advance info, but I heard from my mom that you'll be getting a call this coming week to see if you're interested in becoming the permanent venue. The board raved. And they never rave."

"Really? Wow. That's amazing." She'd had the head's up that it was a possibility, but this sounded like it was confirmed. Could they use it on their website? Surely seeing that they were the permanent home of the Founder's Ball would attract a level of clientele whose fees could offset some of the church groups that wanted to host retreats at Peacock Hill but couldn't quite swing the cost. Deidre would let people come for free, if it was up to her—and Claire got it, but free didn't pay the bills. Heating, cooling, electricity, Internet . . . they all cost money, and those costs increased with groups. Weddings and events like the ball were a great way to set aside money to enable them to offer discounts to church groups. She made a mental note to talk to Deidre about that. "I promise not to let on."

"Well. We were headed up to see Santa. Apparently there's also hot chocolate up there." Topher nudged Vanessa. "It was good to see you."

"Have you given any thought to our conversation, Claire?" Jamie was either ignoring his soon-to-be brother-in-law or he was enjoying Danny's obvious discomfort. Judging by the glint in his eye, it was the latter.

She sighed. "Not yet. I've been a little busy."

"Okay. Well, not to pressure you, but the one job does have a little urgency associated with it." He offered a tight smile before nodding and turning to follow Vanessa and Topher.

Claire swallowed. Why was it that when people said "not to pressure you," they inevitably meant the opposite? "I'm not really in the mood for Santa after all. Do you mind?"

"Nope." Danny turned so they were facing and reached for her hand. "Are you okay?"

"Yes. No. I don't know. Probably?"

He laughed and drew her into his arms. "Should I be jealous?"

"No." Claire tipped her head up and met his gaze. "No, don't be jealous. I thought there was a way for Jamie to help me get over you. But I don't want to get over you. Not if I don't need to."

He brushed his lips across hers. "I don't want you to get over me either. Ever."

Ever? She searched his gaze, and everything in her warmed. He'd said he loved her, and she loved him, but there'd still been a small part of her that wondered and worried. Now, looking into his eyes, she saw the possibility of forever. She leaned up so their lips met.

"Get a room." The mocking tone, followed by laughter jolted Claire back. She turned, shaking her head at the group of teens snickering and slapping one another on the back.

Danny chuckled and slid his arm around her shoulders. "Come on. Let's go see the greenhouse. If I remember correctly, there should be carolers somewhere around there as well."

14

Danny shrank under Mrs. Patterson's steady gaze as he climbed the steps to church. What was it about her that sent him back to being a little boy who was thinking about mischief? He forced a polite smile and nodded as he reached her. "Good morning, Mrs. Patterson."

"I hear you're dating Claire now."

His smile broadened. "Yes, ma'am."

Her nod was brisk. "About time. See you treat her right."

"Yes, ma'am." She didn't seem to have anything more to add, so he slipped past and into the foyer. It was early enough that not many people were milling around, but a few of the youth were busy refilling the prayer cards and exchanging dull pencils for sharp ones in the sanctuary. The smell of slightly burned coffee wafted up from the fellowship hall downstairs. Maybe there was something he could do down there.

Claire looked up from the snack table as he got to the end of the steps. She lit up. "Hey, you."

"Hey, yourself. You're early."

"I guess that makes you the pot and me the kettle. At least I have a reason. Deidre signed us up to bring the after-service snacks and make the coffee."

"Why is it always burned?"

Claire laughed and reached for his hand. She tugged him closer and pressed a quick kiss to his lips. "Because the serving urns are older than either of us. Maybe older than both of us combined. I think after there's been that much coffee run through something, it can't help but hang on to the taste of coffee gone by. If you get a cup right after it's brewed, it's not as bad."

Interesting. He didn't usually get here early enough to test that theory. Most Sundays, he was sneaking in halfway through the singing portion of the worship service. "Think it's too late?"

She shook her head and gestured to the pot. "Give it a shot. But don't touch the cookies. Deidre laid them out just so and I have a feeling she'd pitch a fit if something was out of place. I know it's pregnancy and hormones and whatever, but I don't know how we're supposed to survive around her for another two months."

Was there a safe way to respond to that? "I guess I haven't noticed."

Claire's eyebrows lifted but she didn't say anything.

Danny filled a cup with coffee, dumped in some sugar and creamer, and stirred. He sipped.

"Well?"

"Marginally better than it will be after the service." He sipped again. It was still caffeine. "I'm sorry I got you home so late last night. If I'd known you had to be here to set up, I wouldn't have suggested dessert after we finished the gardens."

She shook her head. "I didn't mention it on purpose. I had a good time, Danny. I like spending time with you. Always have."

"So you were just hanging out with a friend, huh?" He grinned, remembering the hoots and catcalls of the teens who'd passed them on the path when they were kissing. "I'm just one of the guys?"

"Maybe it's a little different now." Cheeks pink, Claire held up her thumb and index finger with a tiny space between them.

Danny chuckled. "Oh, well then, if it's that different."

"Aren't you two done flirting yet?" Deidre, scowl etched on her face, stomped in from the kitchen. "There's stuff to do. I was trying to let you get it out of your system, but we have like five minutes before people start sniffing around."

Claire angled so her face wasn't visible to Deidre and widened her eyes, mouthing, "See what I mean?"

"How can I help, Dee?" Danny fought a laugh at Claire's exaggerated facial expressions. "You look lovely this morning."

"Please. I look like a whale that's trying too hard. And there are two more months and I don't know if any of us are going to make it and still be sane." She burst into tears and waddled back into the kitchen.

"Um." Danny glanced at Claire. "Did I . . .?"

Claire shook her head. "No. That's been happening a lot more lately."

"Is it normal?"

"How am I supposed to know? I've never been pregnant. I mean, she's not wrong. As little as she is, that baby's had nowhere to go but out. So she is enormous. She's still beautiful —she has the pregnancy glow down pat—but I'm pretty sure no one and nothing is going to convince her of it."

The whole conversation was a landmine. A landmine in a swamp full of quicksand. Even if he didn't step on something that was going to explode, it was just as likely that he'd end up getting sucked under and drowning. He cleared his throat. "What else needs to be done for set up down here?"

Claire made a sound halfway between a grunt and a laugh. "Nothing. We're ready. Come on, let's go upstairs. Dee's not going to come back out after that, not even once she gets herself under control. She'll avoid you for the next twenty-four hours if recent experience is a guide."

Danny took Claire's hand as they climbed the stairs. "Is that normal?"

"I have no idea." She frowned. "It's been getting worse since Thanksgiving, though."

Aha. "Your parents?"

"I guess." Claire puffed out her cheeks and blew out the air. "I didn't actually put that together. Stress plus pregnancy is probably a bad combination."

"More than likely." Neither of them was handling this thing with their parents very well. Claire was ignoring it, as if that would make it go away. And if Deidre was randomly exploding, it didn't seem like she was doing all that well either. "How's Duncan doing?"

"I don't know. With everything going on with Anna . . . I don't know." Claire pinched the bridge of her nose. "Maybe after church I'll see if I can bring it up with them. But I don't know what to say. And I guess it means I'll have to bail on doing something with you. Sorry. I mean, we didn't actually have plans yet, but I was hoping . . ."

"Don't worry about it. This is more important."

Claire stopped just inside the sanctuary.

Matt and Azure were sitting in the usual place where the gang from Peacock Hill gathered on Sunday mornings. Danny started down the aisle, stopping as Claire pulled his arm.

"Can we sit back here? Alone?"

"Of course." He followed behind as Claire slipped into the back row and sat in the far corner. What was he supposed to do to help? Was there anything he *could* do? He slid his arm around her shoulders and squeezed. "It's going to be okay."

"You don't know that. No one does."

Danny's heart broke for her again. He leaned over and kissed her temple. "Okay. It may not end up looking like you want it to, but at some point down the line, if you'll let Him, God's going to use this for His good."

Claire frowned. "How is any of this good? How is my parents divorcing and Anna losing a baby good? For any of us?"

"It's good if you let it bring you closer to Him. And it's good if you let Him use it to bring others to Him. We all want those verses in Romans to mean we end up happy and free from pain, but I'm pretty sure that's not what Paul's saying. He's just saying that God will use everything we go through to help us and others draw near to Him if we're willing." Danny rubbed her shoulder. "Which isn't super encouraging in the moment. I'm sorry."

Claire leaned her head against his arm. "It's okay. At least you're not trying to fix it."

"If I could? If I had any idea how? I would be."

She shifted so their eyes met. "Thanks."

Danny hadn't ever wished to be Mr. Fixit more than in that moment. All he could think to do was pray for her and her siblings. So he did.

THE DINER DID a bustling business on Sundays after church. It'd been a while since Danny had fought for space at the counter, but he wasn't going to intrude on a McIntyre family meeting. There was a lot going on that they needed to talk through. He sent up another quick prayer for them to have clarity and patience with one another.

"There you go, hon. Enjoy." Myra was an older woman who'd been serving at the diner for as long as he could remember. She called everyone hon and snapped her gum when she walked between stations taking orders and refilling drinks. She was a little piece of home that he'd miss if she ever decided to retire.

"Thanks." Danny breathed in the rich, meaty scent of his meatloaf and mashed potatoes. A scoop of green beans rounded out the plate and gave the appearance of healthiness. They weren't his favorite, but if he mixed them in with the potatoes, they weren't bad.

"Is this seat taken?"

Danny glanced over and his eyebrows lifted as Jamie Fisher slid onto the stool beside him. "I actually think it might be. There was someone sitting there a minute ago."

Jamie snorted. "Nice try. The woman up front pointed over here. Said it just opened up. What's that? It any good?"

"Meatloaf, and yes. It's one of their specialties." Danny frowned down at his plate, his appetite gone. He cut off a corner of the meatloaf slice, swiped it through the extra gravy on his plate and put it in his mouth. Maybe if he focused on eating, he'd avoid saying things he'd later regret.

"Sounds good." Jamie pushed the menu back into its spot between the sugar and napkins. "So. How'd you enjoy the lights at the botanical gardens last night?"

Really? Danny bit back a sigh. "We had a great time. What about you? Did you get over to the carolers in the greenhouse? They were good."

"Hmm. Must have missed them. My sister spent an inordinate amount of time petting reindeer. Almost like she was trying to keep us from bumping into you two again." Jamie paused when Myra slid a glass of water in front of him.

"What can I get you, hon?"

"I'll have the meatloaf." Jamie jerked a thumb toward Danny's plate.

Danny curved an arm around his food.

"Can't go wrong. You need anything, Dan?"

He shook his head. "No, thanks. I'm good."

She nodded and tore a sheet off her pad before clipping it in line for the cook.

"Come here a lot?" Jamie took a drink of his water and winced.

Danny smothered a smile. "I grew up here. You get to know people over time. That's tap water. It takes some getting used to —we have a high mineral content."

Jamie slid the glass to the back of the counter. "So. You and Claire are . . ."

"Dating." Danny took another bite.

"Mmm. Recent development?"

"You could probably look at it that way. I see it more as the inevitable progression of multiple years of friendship and attraction.'

"Inevitable, huh? So not something you went after, just something you fell into?"

"That's not what I said."

"Didn't you? Sounds like neither of you actually chose this relationship."

"Only if you're not listening closely. We're together. In love. You missed out."

Jamie's face and neck flushed bright red. "I'm not sure you're the one that gets to make that decision."

Danny nodded. "You have a point. Claire knows her own mind. And she chose me."

"Did she, though? Because she's still talking to me about moving to DC and working in my company. Has she even mentioned that to you?"

She hadn't. Not really. Not in the "what should we do about this because my decision impacts both of us" kind of way that couples should talk about things like that.

Jamie smirked. "That's what I figured."

"She has a lot going on right now. I don't think your job offer is as high on her list as you think it is." Danny signaled for Myra. He slipped his wallet out of his pocket and pulled out his last twenty, grateful he'd pulled out cash before his date with Claire.

"Whatcha need, hon?" She snapped her gum.

"Can I get a box and the check?"

"Everything okay?" She reached under the counter and produced a take home container before flipping through her tickets for his bill.

"Yeah. Just a little crowded in here." His gaze slid towards Jamie. "It's giving me indigestion."

Jamie snorted.

Myra nodded and set down his ticket. "See you around, Dan."

"Thanks." He slapped the twenty on the check. It was more than he'd normally tip, but it wasn't outrageous. Anything that got him out of there and away from Jamie Fisher faster was worth doing. He scraped his food into the box, flipped the lid closed, and slid off his stool. "Gotta run."

"Uh huh. You do that. Women always find retreat so attractive."

Danny's grip on the box tightened. "Listen up, Jamie. Claire chose me. She's going to keep choosing me. And if that changes, I'll respect her enough to believe she knows her mind and let her go."

"So you're not going to fight for her?"

Danny offered a sharp grin. "I don't have to. I've already won."

15

C laire picked up her dishes and stacked them on top of Duncan's. She reached for Anna's.

"I can get it." Anna started to rise.

"It's fine. I've got it." Claire continued stacking dishes. Anything to delay the inevitable. This family meeting had been her idea. Anna and Duncan had agreed quickly enough, so it wasn't as if they didn't understand the need, but it was still going to end up being her show. She carried the dishes into the kitchen and set them in the sink.

"This is nice. We should do it once a month—family lunch after church." Deidre scooted her chair back a bit and stretched. "We can rotate homes. It's a nice change from being in the main dining room, too. You've done a great job with your place, Claire."

Claire's eyebrows lifted. Deidre was obviously feeling insecure. She rambled when that happened. "Thanks. You helped a lot."

Pink tinged Dee's cheeks and she reached for Jeremiah's hand.

Claire curled her fingers around the top of the chair she'd

been sitting in. "Do we want to move to the living room? I think my couch is more comfortable."

"I'll never get out of it." Deidre sighed. "Can we just sit here?"

Claire shrugged and glanced at Duncan and Anna. "You two okay with that? You got the weird chairs."

"It's fine." Anna wiggled and the office chair she was in rolled a little closer to the table. "Right, Duncan?"

Duncan shrugged. "Sure. I'm good wherever."

Okay. So. At the table it was. Claire slid back into her seat and folded her hands in her lap. She glanced at Deidre and raised her eyebrows, hoping her sister would take the hint and lead things off.

Dee gave a tiny shake of her head.

"All right. I think we all know why we're here. Mom and Dad."

Heads around the table nodded.

Claire waited. Didn't anyone have something to say? Their gazes rested on her, expectant. "Well, I mean, what are we doing about that? We're not sitting idly by while they destroy our family, are we?"

"What do you propose?" Duncan reached for Anna's hand. "Seriously? They're adults. What exactly are we supposed to do? Forbid them from divorcing?"

"Why not?" Deidre leaned forward. "Are they even thinking this through? How many lectures did they give while we were growing up about the sanctity of marriage and how leaving wasn't an option?"

"Who can count that high?" Duncan shrugged. "But that was then."

"So, what, the kids leave home and magically the rules change? Nope. Life doesn't work that way." Deidre banged her fist on the table then hunched her shoulders. "Sorry."

"It's okay." The table was from a thrift store and had probably been banged on before. Claire cast around for words. "Do you think saying something—having this conversation with them—would help? I didn't . . . I don't know what y'all said at Thanksgiving."

Duncan narrowed his eyes. "You knew."

Claire shrank back from the vitriol in his tone.

"You knew and you didn't say anything?" Hurt flashed in Deidre's eyes.

"What would it have changed?" Claire sank against the back of her chair even as she bristled. "And I didn't know for sure. Not one hundred percent. I figured they were just fighting. You know Mom used to throw out the idea of leaving when she got really ticked."

Deidre drew in a breath but her words were cut off when Jeremiah covered her hands with his.

"It wasn't Claire's news to tell. Stop and think. Really think. Would you have said something?" Jeremiah held Deidre's gaze until she looked away and muttered.

"What was that?" Duncan leaned forward.

Anna shushed him. "You heard her fine. I'm with Jeremiah— I don't know what I would've done in that situation. I want to be annoyed with you, Claire, because it's easier. You're here and an easy target. But really, it's your mom and dad who are the problem, and from where I'm sitting I think the suggestion to go and talk to them about this directly is a good one."

"You do?" Duncan frowned at Anna. "Why?"

"Because everyone was shell shocked at Thanksgiving and no one said anything. Not really. Deidre and Claire should go."

"Why not all three of us? Or all five?" Deidre scowled. "I don't see why I have to go if it's not everyone heading up there. There's stuff to do here."

There wasn't really, but Claire was good with that as an excuse if it would fly. Maybe if she hung back, they'd come up with something else. Anything else. The absolute last thing Claire wanted to do was go to DC and talk to her parents. Would they even agree to it?

"I can man the fort." Jeremiah rubbed Deidre's arm. "Everything is slowing down for Christmas right now. Even if I get a few calls to come hang lights, I'm sure I can handle that and whatever's going on here. What *is* going on here?"

Claire sighed as everyone shifted to look at her. "Nothing until the weekend. We have different groups Friday, Saturday, and Sunday, but nothing else this week."

"There are repairs . . . and okay, they're not urgent. What about the baby?" Deidre rested a hand on her stomach.

"You'd be going to DC. Driving. There are arguably better and closer hospitals up there if you have an issue." Anna nodded firmly, as if that settled everything.

"I still don't see why Duncan isn't also coming." Deidre pouted.

"I need him here." Anna visibly swallowed. "I can't—you have to stay."

Duncan shot Deidre a pointed look.

Claire nearly winced herself from the poison in it. It was probably bad form for Deidre to have tried to use her baby as an excuse when Anna had just lost hers. "I could go by myself. I guess."

"No. I'll come. If you go, no one will know what was said. You'll just decide to keep it to yourself in case they aren't serious."

"Dee. That was uncalled for." Jeremiah sent his wife a quelling look. "But I do think it's a good idea for the two of you to go. Your parents can't brush off both of you."

Sure they could. They were great at that. Or they always had been when she and Dee were kids. Maybe now that they were adults their parents would recognize that there needed to be some modicum of respect. She fought a snort. Right.

"Fine." Deidre glared at Claire. "I can't go tomorrow. Tuesday works."

"Okay. Want to meet them for lunch? Maybe you could arrange to meet Dad and I'll ask Mom?"

"Sneaky. Yeah, okay." Dee huffed out a breath. "I'm still not sure this is going to do anything."

Neither was Claire, but what else were they supposed to do? Sit back and let their parents destroy years of marriage and family? Just because marriage didn't seem to have a lot of value in the culture at large didn't mean Christians weren't supposed to be different. Better. "It's something to try."

"Maybe after we could do a little shopping?" Claire's face must have shown her feelings on that, clearly, because Deidre hurried on, "Or you could drop me at the mall for an hour? Two, tops? I love living here, but ordering everything online gets old. I could probably make a trip to Charlottesville or Richmond, but we'll be up in DC—you know that's going to be better."

Claire gave a grudging nod. "I can park myself in a coffee shop and wait for you."

Anna laughed. "You don't like shopping at all?"

"If I have something I need, sure. But unlike Queen Dee over there, I actually enjoy doing that shopping online."

"Queen Dee?" Laughing, Jeremiah looked at his wife. "That's new."

"No. It's old. And dead. And the last time she called me that, my response left a bruise that lasted over a week. So keep that in mind." Deidre's eyes shot daggers.

"Sorry. Couldn't help myself." Claire cleared her throat. "Any other news we need to discuss?"

Duncan glanced around the table. "Well, I think we'd all like to know what's going on with you and Danny."

Heat suffused her face. "What do you think's going on?"

They all laughed.

Deidre reached over to pat Claire's arm. "I'm glad. It's about time. You two are a good fit."

Claire smiled. They were and they weren't. They'd been friends a long time. Then they'd been . . . not friends. Going from actively pushing herself to stop wanting anything to do with Danny to letting herself love him was odd. Not bad. But there were moments here and there where she asked herself what she was doing.

~

"HI, DAD." Deidre levered herself up off the bench in front of the restaurant where they'd agreed to meet.

Claire stood and nodded toward the door. "Why don't the two of you go in, I'll be just another second."

So far, at least, things were going according to plan. They'd staggered their parents' arrival times in hopes of keeping one of them from spotting the other and storming off in a huff. Of course, there was no guarantee that the public place would prevent a scene, but it was a risk they'd have to take. Since only their parents still lived up here, the fallout was minimal to either Claire or Dee.

It was a full five minutes after Dad and Dee disappeared inside that her mother clipped up the sidewalk. Claire's eyebrows lifted. Gone was the mother she remembered. In her place was a woman clearly on the hunt for a man. Her skirt skimmed just above her knee enough that it said "older woman trying too hard." The bolero jacket and enormous purse that begged for some kind of small animal to peek out of it completed the outfit.

"Hi, darling. This is such a nice surprise."

Claire stood. "Mom. You look interesting."

Her mother laughed. "I'm finding myself, dear. There are bound to be a few missteps."

"Were you lost?" Claire regretted the quip as soon as it left her mouth.

Her mother angled her head and sighed. "Not lost, so much as settled. There's such a thing as everything being too easy. It's difficult to understand at your age, Claire. I know that. But I don't want to look back at the end of my life and realize that I never knew what passion was."

"So what? Our family was boring? Duty?"

"Convenient." Her mother's fingers drifted lightly over Claire's arm. "Your father was just always there—even before we dated. He was there, in the background, waiting for his chance. That's what he'd always say. And I knew he'd always be there. He's steady. Stable. And I convinced myself that that was what I needed. What I wanted. There were never fireworks with your father, but I also knew I'd never want for anything. Now, I realize that was unfair to both of us. Shall we go in?"

Frozen in place, Claire could scarcely breathe. Her thoughts spun too quickly for her to grab any of them. Except one. This lunch was a terrible, terrible idea.

And there was no way to stop the impending disaster.

Her mother turned at the door. "Aren't you coming?"

"Yeah." Claire pushed her feet forward and tried to affix a smile. "You're not putting a dog in that purse are you?"

The restaurant was busy. It was a popular place for office workers who wanted a longer, more interesting lunch than fast food. Managers in suits and ties wheeled and dealed in booths with clients and higher ups. And tucked in the corner were her father and Deidre.

Dee had been smart enough to make her father slide in first.

Less chance of him pushing his pregnant daughter to the floor in an attempt to run away.

Claire's mom froze and shot Claire a scathing glare over her shoulder before striding to the table. "Well. Isn't this a lovely surprise? Deidre, you look positively enormous."

"Mom!" Claire grabbed her mother's arm and dug in, her voice lowering to a harsh whisper. "Do you think this is easy for any of us? Did you think you could just destroy everything without your children getting involved? You want this? Be an adult and explain yourself. Politely."

Her mother gaped for a moment before offering a short nod and sliding into the booth. "I apologize, Deidre, you're lovely and you know it. I will state for the record that I don't appreciate being ambushed."

"Hear, hear." Her father raised his glass of soda and took a long drink. "What is it, exactly, the two of you are hoping to accomplish?"

"We'd like to understand." Deidre's voice was calmer than Claire would've been able to manage.

Mom and Dad exchanged looks. Dad leaned back in the banquette and gestured for Mom to proceed. "I'd like that, myself."

Claire studied her father across the table. He was pale. Thinner. And he looked tired. He didn't want this any more than she and her siblings did, did he? So why wasn't he fighting? Wouldn't that be the passion Mom was looking for? Why was he just letting her have her way?

"I'm not positive anything I say will help you. Any of you. I realized that there was a lot missing from my life and that if I was going to do more than simply exist through my golden years, it was going to be up to me to go after what I needed. When I chose to marry your father, I based a lot of that choice on a desire for stability. Stable is something he's always been, so I settled. I've never been happy—truly happy—and I think if you're all honest, you'll realize that. So all of this? It's me changing my circumstances so I can be happy."

"Didn't you tell us that happiness was something you chose?" Deidre looked at Claire. "Didn't she?"

"She did. It was one of many parenting lecture themes. Happiness and love are choices you make on a daily basis. You can be happy in any circumstance and situation, because you have joy in your relationship with Jesus." Claire held up a finger as her mother prepared to speak. "It went along with how happiness was not the point of life. The point of life was living in faithful obedience to Christ and how that brought richer, deeper rewards than fleeting happiness."

Pink tinged her mother's cheeks, visible even in the lowered lights of the restaurant.

A smirk hovered on her father's lips. "Indeed."

"I said you weren't going to understand, and I meant it." Claire's mom straightened her shoulders. "Besides, your father isn't exactly doing anything to stop this."

"What do you propose I do, exactly? Lock you in a bedroom? Disable the cars? You brought this to me as a done deal. 'Inevitable' is, I believe, the word you chose. Who am I to stand in the way of your happiness?" Her father shrugged and sipped his soda again. "And I did suggest counseling. I want credit for that."

"That's a great idea. You could talk with the pastor—or maybe at this point someone with full credentials would be better." Deidre drew her phone out of her purse and started tapping. "It should be easy enough to find someone who can help you both individually and together."

Dad reached over and covered Dee's phone, pushing it down on the table. "She said no."

Deidre blinked and pinned their mom with a glare. "You won't even try?"

Mom's eyes narrowed like they'd shoot lasers if they could.

Before she could speak, the server, impossibly chipper, stopped at their table with a refill for Dad and to get drink and food orders for everyone else. She disappeared with a promise to bring out a basket of bread.

"That's how you're going to play it?" Mom looked across at Dad and shook her head. "Typical."

"What's typical? I told the truth. I offered—we could say begged—to go to counseling. You said no, your mind was made up. There was nothing to be gained." Dad spread his hands. "That's not 'playing it.' It's reporting facts."

"You're going to sit there and tell me you're happy?"

Dad shook his head. "Never said that. The truth is, since I retired and the kids moved away, it's been an adjustment. But that's what I was doing. Adjusting. I thought that's what you were doing, too."

Mom looked triumphant. "See? No one in this marriage is happy."

"True. But I never said happiness had become my god. There've been a lot of times in my life when I've been unhappy. Long seasons, here and there. And those talking points Claire parroted back a few minutes ago? They've gotten me through."

Claire's eyes filled. Dad sounded so defeated. Why didn't her mother see it? Hear it? "When did you get so self-absorbed?"

"I beg your pardon?" Her mother shifted and frowned at Claire. "You will not speak to me like that. I'm still your mother."

"Biologically, sure. Beyond that? Nope. If you're doing this, I'm done. I won't stand by and watch you destroy my father and the family that I love. And you seem content to do just that in search of this idea that there's something else out there—something newer and shinier—that's going to make you happy. Here's a tip: if you aren't happy with yourself? Nothing external is ever going to change that." Claire slid from the booth and looked at Deidre. "I can wait in the car."

Deidre shook her head and wiggled free from the table. "No. It's fine. I'm ready to go, too. I expected more. From both of you."

"What about your food?" Dad slid toward the end of the booth and stood. "At least see if you can get it boxed up to go."

Claire nodded. "I'll ask at the front. For ours. The two of you can make your own decisions. Come on, Dee."

16

Danny hovered outside the plate glass window that spanned the front of the jewelry store. He'd been spending entirely too much time looking at diamonds and settings online. It was time to look in person.

Probably.

He stuffed his hands in his pockets. It was still too early. That hadn't changed. Had it? Jamie hovering around the diner and trying to lure Claire off to DC—and into his arms—didn't make it the right time to give Claire an engagement ring. What was he doing? He should go back to work. There was plenty to do there. And at least at the office, he knew the right steps to take.

Danny turned and started to trudge back to his car.

"Danny? Hey! Danny!"

He stopped and, after a wince, glanced over his shoulder. "Hey, Sean. What brings you out this way?"

"You mean near one of the best jewelry stores in Charlottesville? It's a professional hazard. What about you?" Sean smirked.

"I just needed to get out of the office for a little air. I was heading back, actually. So. I'll see you." Danny lifted a hand and started walking.

"Dude." Sean jogged up next to Danny and grabbed his arm. "Where are you going?"

"Back to work, I said."

"Uh huh." Sean frowned. "Why don't you come in with me? It's a nice shop. Good people. I could use an extra set of eyes. I'm supposed to get ideas for wedding bands, and I find I don't actually know what I want."

If he knew Sean—which admittedly, he didn't, not super well at least—the guy probably already had exactly what he wanted picked out and just needed to point to it. This was a ploy to get him in the store. And yet, hadn't that been the whole point of coming down here? He sighed. "All right. Larissa doesn't have something in mind? Something that matches?"

Sean shook his head and tugged open the door. "Her engagement ring has a band that attaches to the solitaire, so she's set. I offered to get her another as well, but she's happy with what she has. It's vintage and doesn't really need anything more."

Danny stepped into the jewelry store and looked around. The lighting was subdued and everything felt hushed, like a library. Maybe this place was out of his price range after all. The mall stores never came across this way. They were loud and bright with voices from the food court—why were they always by the food court?—pinging off the walls.

Of course, the mall store also had the same engagement ring everyone got. Claire deserved something more than that. Something special. "You got Larissa a vintage ring?"

"Yeah. There's a shop in Richmond that specializes in estate jewelry. It's not for everyone, but I knew she'd like the idea of having something that had stood the test of time."

"You don't want that for your own band?"

"I never even really considered it. Honestly? I think I'd be happy with a simple gold band, but she wants me to look and be sure. Since I was out here to meet a client for a dress fitting, I figured I'd swing in and then I could at least say I gave it more thought."

Danny nodded and eyed the cases. It was somewhat surprising that they hadn't been accosted by a sales person. At the mall, they jumped in with gleaming, toothy smiles the second your foot crossed into their space. At least that's what it felt like. This was a lot nicer.

He angled closer and took a few steps, eyeing the various offerings.

"Down this way." Sean pointed. "The wedding cases are closer to the back."

Danny chuckled. "I guess you'd know."

"Like I said, professional hazard." Sean stopped and tugged a stool out from where it was tucked under and out of the way. He sat and nodded to the other stool. "Have a seat."

With a mental shrug, Danny lowered himself to the fabric-covered square. The array of rings was larger than seemed reasonable for men's wedding bands. He leaned toward the simple gold band himself. Maybe something subtly etched. But the variety here. He tapped the glass above a ring that sparkled with diamonds. "Do guys actually wear those? That's more glitter than most engagement rings."

Sean grinned. "Some want it, yeah. I guess they figure if their wife gets bling, they should too."

Danny snorted. "Bling. I'm pretty sure no one says that anymore."

"Yeah, well." Sean pointed to a two-tone band in rose gold and something with a brown hue. "I like that."

"It's pink."

"Not very. And I think maybe the dark metal is tungsten. It's different. I like it." Sean glanced around and made eye contact with a salesman.

The older man walked over. "Gentlemen. I'm Neil. How can I help you today?"

"Hi, Neil. I'm Sean. This is Danny. We're friends but not together. I'm looking at wedding bands, and I think Danny was here for engagement rings."

Danny's face heated. He'd thought Sean had let that go. Guess not. He shrugged. "I guess. Since I'm here."

"Very good. Since we're here, what can I show you?"

Sean tapped the glass above the band he'd been eyeing. "Could I see this?"

"Of course. It's a unique look. Rose gold and espresso tungsten with yellow gold accents. Simple, but not boring." The man removed the band, spread out a small rectangle of black velvet on top of the glass, and set the ring on it.

Sean picked it up and ran his thumb along the crease dividing the gold from the tungsten before slipping it on his left hand. It didn't quite slide all the way over his knuckle, but he held out his fingers anyway. "What do you think?"

"It's not as pink on." Danny considered the ring. "It's actually not bad. And it's different but still traditional. Which I guess summarizes you fairly well, doesn't it?"

"It does." He shifted his gaze to Neil. "Is it wrong to look at one and decide that's it?"

Neil shook his head. "Not if you're certain, which it seems you are. Let's measure your finger so we can order the proper size."

Sean took the set of rings Neil offered and tried them until he found one that slipped off and on easily but didn't slide off. "This one."

Neil nodded. "One moment. I can take care of the paperwork

on this if you want to look at the engagement rings for a moment. Did you have something specific in mind?"

Danny shook his head. "I spent too much time looking online. I don't even know what she'd want—there are so many options."

Neil smiled. "Indeed. Why don't you browse. I'll be right with you."

Sean stood and pushed his stool back under the overhang. "You don't have any idea?"

Danny fought the urge to hunch his shoulders. "Not really. Am I supposed to? Does it mean something that I don't?"

"Have you and Claire even talked about marriage?"

Danny stuffed his hands in his pockets and strode down toward the display cases Neil had indicated held engagement rings. "Abstractly."

"Hm."

What did that mean? Danny scowled at the diamonds ranging in size from tiny to eye-popping as they glittered in the case. Claire wouldn't want something outrageous. But . . . did she even like diamonds? More and more women were going for other gemstones in their rings, was she someone who would want to do that? There were a couple of blue stones—sapphires?— surrounded by diamonds in the back of the case that were pretty. "I'm going to have to ask her, aren't I? It can't just be a surprise."

"It could. You could always enlist some help. I mean she has a sister and a sister-in-law right there at Peacock Hill. Between them and Azure you could probably get someone to bring up the conversation and see what she has to say."

That sounded like it could backfire. Badly. Three married women oh-so-casually bringing up engagement rings? He'd be better off just asking her himself. Especially since she wasn't big on surprises in the first place. And having a more on-point conversation about marriage at the same time. Just because that's where his thoughts were heading didn't mean it's what she wanted. Or was ready for. His stomach sank. What if she said it wasn't what she wanted ever?

No. He wasn't going there. Even with the mess her parents were making right now, Claire believed in marriage and knew that's where they were headed.

Didn't she?

"This is dumb. I should go. I thought looking in person would clarify things. I was wrong." Danny rubbed the back of his neck. "I'll just talk to Claire myself. A surprise proposal is a nice idea, but it's not super practical."

"Just because you talk about marriage and engagement rings doesn't mean she knows your timeline. You can still work a surprise, if that's what you want." Sean clapped Danny's shoulder. "I, for one, am glad to see you finally heading this direction. The two of you make a great couple."

"Do we?"

"Of course you do. You've been friends forever, so you know everything about one another and now, you're adding a new layer on top of that foundation. Why are you looking at rings if you don't think you're a good couple?"

"I do. That's not—never mind."

"Danny. You want to go grab some lunch and talk?"

Danny shook his head and checked his watch. "I gotta run. I have a client call I need to finish prepping for. I'll talk to Claire and maybe it'll make more sense."

"Okay. You know you can call me any time, right?"

He smiled. "Yeah. Thanks, man. I like your wedding band— even if it's pink. Think Larissa will like it?"

Sean nodded. "Pretty sure. Guess I should text her a picture though before it's final."

Danny laughed. "Probably so. Later."

He gave a mock salute to Neil as he headed toward the front of the jewelry store. He should have walked faster when Sean first said hello. Going in the store hadn't done anything to answer his questions. If anything, it had raised new ones.

Sean thought they made a good couple. Jeremiah had said the same thing. Danny thought so, too.

Did Claire?

Or was Jamie onto something? Were they only together because Danny didn't want to lose her before he had a chance to see where things led?

He didn't have an answer to that.

And it scared him.

DANNY SLID his personal-sized pizza out of the toaster oven and onto a plate. He wrinkled his nose. He never remembered that the timing on the package was about three minutes too long for his particular appliance, so the crust had some aggressive browning on it. But it was food, and that was all he was going for. Food he didn't have to really do anything to make.

What was the line from the old movie his mom loved about the Australian guy and the New York writer? *Tastes horrible, but you can live on it.* Something like that.

He carried the plate to the living room and set it on the coffee table before dropping onto the couch and clicking on the TV. He hit play for the next episode of the show he was streaming and frowned at the pizza. He was going to need to cut it into pieces.

Danny pushed to his feet and padded back to the kitchen for a knife. Maybe he should have broken down and actually cooked, but the day had been such a complete disaster, he hadn't really been willing to ruin anything else.

The doorbell chimed.

Danny detoured to the front door and dragged it open. He smiled and everything seemed to lighten just a little. "Claire. Hey. Come in."

"Hi. I'm sorry. Should I have called? Or texted? I just . . ."

"No. Please." Danny reached for her hand and pulled her close. "I always want to see you."

Claire rested her head on his shoulder and sighed. "Thanks."

"What's wrong?" Danny shuffled back so he could close the door without releasing Claire. It was chilly out tonight. No sense in letting all the heat out. "Come sit. Have you eaten?"

Claire squeezed him before stepping out of his embrace. "I'm not hungry. You go ahead and eat. I clearly interrupted. You don't mind if I hang?"

"Of course not. I can burn you a pizza if you want."

She snorted out a laugh. "That's an offer."

Danny shrugged, but inside he grinned. For a moment when she'd laughed, the worry etched into her features had disappeared. "Best I can do tonight."

"Your day had to be better than mine." Claire settled on the sofa next to him and raised her eyebrows at the scorched pizza. "Or not if that's actually acceptable dinner fare."

"It's not too bad. And really, this isn't gourmet cuisine. Burned or no, it's not even comparable to delivery. But it's cheap and fast." Gosh, he sounded like a bachelor. Not that he wasn't one, but still, talk about walking into a stereotype. "I *can* cook."

She patted his knee. "I know. I'm just in a weird mood. You eat."

Danny set the knife next to the pizza and hit pause on the TV. "Do you want to talk about it?"

"I don't know. We went to see my parents today—Dee and I. And I didn't have a lot of expectations, but I guess they were still too high, because I just don't understand. It's like my mom has turned into this person I don't even recognize anymore. She's sitting there talking about how she's unhappy and so she had to make changes and my whole life it was always how happiness isn't everything because Jesus didn't promise us that. He just promised to be with us if we were faithful. But now suddenly she feels entitled to easy happiness instead of doing the work to make things right?" Claire threw up her hands. "Where is that even coming from?"

"Everywhere? Seriously, look around. The world is all about happiness and personal fulfillment."

Claire sighed. "I guess. But how do you make such a drastic switch? And my poor dad. I thought he was okay with things, but he isn't. He's just . . . defeated."

Danny slid his arm around her shoulders and pulled her close. What was he supposed to say? He'd been in enough relationships that he knew not to try and fix it—not that he had any solutions beyond not taking it on as something she was supposed to fix. Her parents were adults. This was their issue. But saying that would probably land him in the doghouse, too. Empathy. That was what Casey had always nagged him about. "I'm sorry."

"Thanks. I just . . . I know it's not mine to carry, right? But these are my parents. It feels like I should be able to do something—say something—that would make them see reason. And it turns out my mom won't even go to counseling, even though Dad asked her to. How does that even make sense?"

"I don't know. I can't imagine a situation where I wouldn't want to do anything possible to make things work with you."

Claire tipped her face up, her eyes meeting his. A hint of a smile ghosted around her lips. "I love you."

"I love you, too." Danny brushed his lips over hers. Was now the right time? Maybe it was. "In fact, I wanted to talk to you about something."

She blinked, a tiny crease forming between her eyebrows. "Okay?"

"I—" He stopped and cleared his suddenly clogged throat. "At lunchtime, I was thinking about you, so I got out of the office for a bit and wandered into a jewelry store."

Claire's mouth formed an O, but she didn't speak.

"And I realized I didn't have any idea what sort of jewelry you liked. Like at all. You hardly ever wear any, and I guess it seemed like we should maybe talk about it before I got you something that you didn't like, and Sean was surprised that we hadn't already hashed things out since I was at the store and I don't even know if you like diamonds."

"Sean. Wedding planner Sean. Was at the jewelry store with you?"

"Not on purpose." This was not going the way it should. He couldn't say the way he'd planned, because he hadn't really planned on having the conversation right now. Tonight. He'd planned to spend some time thinking and praying about how to open up the talk. He should have done that. Gah. "He showed up. I was leaving. Then he was all 'come inside with me' and . . . this is a disaster. You had no idea I was even thinking engagement rings, did you?"

"Well. Not really. I mean it's been what, three weeks if we're generous?"

Three weeks. Sure. Officially. "But Claire. Two years."

"Sure. Two years of friendship. Ish. I mean the last what, six, nine months? Were we even friends? Casey didn't love that you hung out with us—with me. Then suddenly you're not with her and you're kissing me and it's enough to make my head spin."

"Is that bad?"

Claire stood and paced across the room. "No. Not bad. Just a lot. And with my parents. I mean, how am I supposed to think about marriage and a lifetime commitment when they're in the process of proving just how unlikely that is? How do I believe it's possible when my mom is willing to walk away from years without a second glance?"

He wanted to go to her. To hold her. But that was probably the wrong move. Why did this whole situation have him second and third and fourth guessing himself? It wasn't right. Or fair. Not that fair really had a place in life, he knew that, but just once it would be nice. "I don't know what to say. I love you. I want a life—a future with you. I can wait, if that's what you want. Need. But I don't want you to give up on me—on us—because someone else decided to give up on her marriage."

"It's my *mom*, Danny. It's not some random person on the street. I know the divorce rate is like half or slightly more. And that's for people who bother to get married. It doesn't take into account all the people our age who just skip that step and then break up ten or fifteen years into things. That's different though. Don't ask me how, or why, it just is."

"I get it." Sort of. "But it doesn't change what I'm saying. Give us a chance, Claire. Please?"

Claire bit her lip and met his gaze. "How do I do that and still chase my dreams?"

"What do you mean?" He stilled, almost afraid to move, as fear churned greasily in his stomach.

"I have a job offer. I told you, didn't I? In DC. It's . . . I don't know how to turn it down. It's everything I could possibly want. Plus insurance and stability—no more wondering if we're going to get enough bookings to make things work. Not that Peacock Hill is in trouble. It isn't. Especially not since the Founder's Ball. That was a big help—we're getting a lot of calls. We may even end up turning people away. But that's now. What happens in six months? Ten? A year? There's no guarantee that it'll last."

"And your corporate job comes with a guarantee?" He

clamped his lips shut. Too late. He shouldn't have said it. He could tell from the stony expression on her face.

"No. No guarantee. But it's got more of one than a small operation like Peacock Hill. I don't expect you to understand. You straddle the line, living down here in the middle of nowhere but commuting up to the city for your own corporate job. Not everyone gets the best of both worlds. Most of us have to choose. And I've spent all my life basing my choices on what other people asked me to do. At some point—and I'm thinking now—I'd like to make a decision for myself."

"Then that's what you should do." Danny balled his hands into fists in his lap. "I wouldn't ever ask you to be someone or do something contrary to who you are—to who God made you to be. If you need to go to DC to figure that out, then you should do that."

Confusion and hurt flashed across her features before resolving into determination. She nodded. "I had planned to wait until Dee gave birth. Maybe I shouldn't."

Every word was like a pickaxe chipping away at his heart. But he wasn't going to be accused of manipulation. Or coercion. He forced a smile. "If there's a way for me to help, let me know."

"What?"

He shrugged. "Moving or loading the car or whatever. If I can help, I will."

"Right. Good. Thanks." Claire glanced around the room and nodded toward the coffee table. "Your pizza's probably cold."

"That's okay. It can be reheated." Not that he would. It was headed for the trash. There was no way he was going to be able to force food into his stomach the way it was twisted into knots. Had they just broken up? He wasn't going to ask, but it sure sounded like it to him. And that left him where? "Can you stay or do you need to get back?"

Claire blinked. "Oh. Um. I guess I should get back. Now that

I know what I'm doing, there's a lot to get organized. If I work at it, maybe I could head up on Saturday and start the job Monday. I'll need to reach out to Jamie and see what he wants."

What Jamie wants? Danny fought the growl that started in his chest. Jamie wanted *her*. How did she not see that? He pushed to his feet. "Of course. I guess I'll see you when I see you."

"Danny . . ." Claire stepped close and searched his face. She cupped his cheek. "I need to do this for me. So I don't end up with regrets later. Regrets that turn into reasons for destroying the life I have."

He nodded. If that helped her get through the day, then she might as well think it. There were ways to navigate regrets that didn't involve walking away from anything, but she didn't see it right now. Probably couldn't see it. Just like she didn't see his heart breaking.

"I love you."

He covered her hand with his. "I love you too."

"I'm glad you understand." Claire kissed him and headed for the door.

Danny closed his eyes and listened to the click of the front door as it closed behind her.

Nothing before had ever sounded so final.

17

C laire closed the lid of the trunk and stepped back.

"You're all packed?" Deidre crossed her arms on top of her belly and didn't bother to wipe at the tears streaming down her cheeks.

"Yeah. I appreciate you letting me keep the apartment. If you hire someone and they need it before I find a permanent place in DC, just say the word and I'll come move the rest of my stuff into storage." Claire dusted her hands on her jeans and looked beyond her sister at the gleaming white mansion that had been her home for a while now. "You've done an amazing job with this place, and people have noticed. You're not going to have any trouble keeping things going."

"You don't know that." Deidre swiped at her cheeks. "We need you, Claire. I need you. For more than the event planning and organization. You know that. I know you know it. You just don't care."

"Don't you get it? I need to do this for me. I've worked for you my whole adult life. It's time I find out if I'm actually good at my job, or just good at being your sister."

Deidre blinked. "You've lost your mind. How can you even wonder that?"

"Mom spent her whole—"

"Don't." Deidre held up her hand. "Don't bring Mom into this. And if you're doing this because of Mom, then you're not as smart as I thought you were. Tell me this isn't all about Mom."

"It's not. Not all of it." She'd been thinking about it—looking into new jobs—before she'd found out about Mom and Dad. Of course, that had been motivated in large part by a need to get away from Danny, since it seemed like he was going to end up with Casey. Now . . . well, now she really did need to do this for herself. She'd started the ball rolling and she needed to see where it led.

"Uh huh. What does Danny say about all of this?"

"He said he understood." Claire frowned when her sister snorted. "What?"

"I thought you said the two of you were serious."

"We are. We're fine. People have long distance relationships all the time."

"Sure. For a month. Until they realize it's ridiculous. This isn't you taking a sabbatical. You're moving. For a job. Permanently."

Permanently? "It doesn't have to be forever."

"Does your job know that? Was the offer for a short-term hire? How long? Six months? A year?"

"Why are you being like this? There's no end date on the job, but there's no guarantee, right? Maybe I won't like it. Or they'll decide I'm not a good fit. Anything could happen. That doesn't mean I don't want to try."

"Where are you going to live?"

"I don't know yet. I'll find something once I'm up there. For now, they pay enough I can do one of those extended stay places without it being too awful."

"Claire."

"What? I don't know, okay? I don't have all the details ironed out yet."

"And still you're jumping in your car with everything you need to live and diving in."

Claire bristled. "Just because you've morphed into a stick in the mud doesn't mean all of us have to. Or do you not remember buying this place essentially sight unseen and moving down here with a pocketful of wishes and not much else?"

"That's different."

"How? How is it different?" Claire crossed her arms and tapped her foot. Just let her sister try and talk her way out of it. The only difference was that Deidre had been striking out on her own, away from corporate influence and security, and Claire was running toward it.

Deidre blew out a breath. "Okay. Fine. It's not all that different. But at least I left room for you in my dreams. You're leaving everyone and everything behind."

"I have to. I wish you'd understand that. I don't want to turn sixty and realize I don't know who I am."

Deidre snorted.

"You know it's possible. Look at Mom."

"Mom's delusional."

Claire lifted a shoulder. She mostly agreed, but there was a tiny sliver that could—almost—understand where her mother was coming from. Almost. And she didn't want to end up there, looking back over her life and realizing that she'd never done anything but settle.

Deidre looked away. "You should go. It's a long drive and you don't want to unpack in the dark. Danny isn't coming to see you off?"

"I didn't tell him I was leaving today."

"Claire."

The censure in her sister's voice had Claire hunching her shoulders. "What? He's at work. And he has a big client right now that's giving him some fits. I didn't want to pull him away when he needs not to be distracted. I'll call him later and let him know. Maybe he can come up over the weekend."

Deidre shook her head.

"It's fine. He's fine with it. We're fine."

"Keep saying 'fine', maybe you'll convince yourself."

Claire frowned and rounded the car before yanking open the driver's side door. "I'll let you know when I'm there."

"Whatever." Deidre lifted a hand before she turned and started up the steps to the front door.

Claire watched her sister leave and slumped against the steering wheel. She was doing the right thing. Danny hadn't said otherwise. He'd understood. He hadn't tried to talk her out of it at all. That was because he got it, wasn't it? She needed to do this. For herself. For her relationship with Danny. Just . . . for everything.

If she was going to stand on her own two feet, she had to give them a chance to support her weight.

"YOU SURE YOU want to stay here?" Jamie tipped his head back and eyed the dilapidated extended stay hotel. "This doesn't seem like the safest neighborhood. I have plenty of room, and we could carpool to the office. Plus, since we're working together anyway, it'd be great to be able to get a hold of you whenever."

Yeah, there was no way that would fly. Not with her parents. Not with Deidre. Certainly not with Danny. Even if Claire was on board with it, which she wasn't. When she left work for the day, she wanted to leave work. That was one of the big draws of a corporate job. There were distinct hours that you worked and then there was free time. So much of the time at Peacock Hill, work was anytime, anywhere, because if Dee got a thought, she'd walk over and knock on the door. "It's temporary. I've got some feelers out for a place of my own. Worst case, I end up here 'til the new year. That's what, three weeks? And I'll be back down at Peacock Hill for five days at Christmas. This is fine."

"I guess. If you change your mind, let me know. The offer stands. Indefinitely."

The gleam in his eye had Claire taking a step back. "Jamie. You know I'm with Danny, right?"

"Are you?" He took a step closer. The distance between them was the same as it had been, but it was claustrophobic.

She stepped back again, running into one of the columns of the portico. "I am. We are. This is just work. Weekends, holidays, I'll be back down there. And it's only a couple of hours. In the long run, we'll figure out what we need to do. For now, the distance isn't going to be an issue."

"It's tough. The long distance thing."

"Yeah, well, Danny's worth it."

"Is he?'

"Yes. Of course he is. What kind of question is that?"

"An honest one. Don't you wonder why he's suddenly interested in you when, from what I can tell, he wanted anyone but you for the longest time?"

"No." She absolutely didn't. Wasn't going to start, either. She and Danny had something solid. Something special. They had a foundation of friendship underpinning their love, and a little bit of distance wasn't going to do anything but make that stronger.

Jamie held up his hands. "Okay. I think it's great that you were able to convince him to let you come up here. Especially with your relationship so new. I mean, he's gotta be upset. But you stood firm in the face of his arguments. That's good."

"He didn't argue. He understood that I needed to do this. For me."

Jamie laughed, then sobered. "You're serious?"

"Yes. Because he's a gentleman and would never pressure me to do something that went against what I needed to do." Would he even get the subtle dig? Probably not. Jamie wasn't the most self-aware man she'd ever run into.

He shook his head. "I'd fight for you. You deserve that."

"I think I deserve a man who isn't threatened by me needing to try new things." It was good Danny hadn't pushed. She was susceptible to guilt—it was her mother's favorite tool, guilt and manipulation—Danny respected her. He loved her. She wasn't going to let Jamie sow seeds of doubt about their relationship.

"If you say so."

"I do. Look, I appreciate you coming to help unload my car, but I think maybe I'll take a rain check on dinner. I have all the start up information in my email. I know where to go on Monday and what time. So I think I'm set." If Jamie was going to pester her about Danny, this new job was going to be less wonderful than she'd thought. Hopefully he'd leave off at the office. He could be professional, right?

"Don't be that way. Let me take you out. A welcome home dinner. You can be in charge of all the conversational topics." He drew an X over his heart. "Promise."

Claire shook her head. She wanted to trust him. Wanted to believe that they could have a cordial, friendly relationship. The kind of relationship she'd thought she'd made clear she was open to. But right now, pizza in her suite sounded like the safer, saner option. "It's been a long day. I really do appreciate the help unloading."

Jamie tucked his hands in his pockets and sighed. "If you're sure. I guess I'll see you Monday?"

Would she? HR and inprocessing should take most of the

day, shouldn't it? And the job she'd accepted wasn't the one that interfaced directly with Jamie. "I guess we'll see. Night."

Claire stepped quickly through the lobby doors and headed for the elevator. At least all the suite entrances were on inside hallways. One of the first places she'd looked at had outside access. This place was worth the extra twenty bucks a day to have that little extra bit of security.

Her phone buzzed with a text as she swiped her card to unlock her room. She glanced down and chewed her lip.

Danny.

She went inside, flipping the light switch and bolting the extra locks before glancing around her space. It was clean. So it had that going for it. That was about all it had going for it. Grey and beige were the primary colors in the fabrics on the rock hard loveseat and curtains in the sitting room slash kitchenette. The bedroom was literally that. A room with a bed. But she hadn't been wrong with what she'd told Jamie. This was temporary. Three weeks. Maybe four. She would surely be able to lock in an apartment in that amount of time. Even working.

Ignoring the text, she thumbed open a web browser and found a pizza delivery place nearby. After a quick call to place an order, she settled on the uncomfortable sofa and tapped Danny's message.

You up for dinner?

Claire winced. She hadn't actually gotten around to letting him know she'd left a day earlier than her initial plan. The longer she put it off, the less sure she was about how to say it. When she'd left his place on Tuesday, things had been strained. Sure, he'd been supportive, but she could tell he was upset. And they'd never really gotten back to the conversation about engagement rings.

They hadn't spoken since.

A few texts here and there, but nothing important. Nothing

that meant anything. Claire had planned to give him time to lick his wounds and let his heart match up with the understanding words he'd said. Deep down, he had to know this was the right thing for her. They'd figure out how to navigate a long distance relationship.

They had to.

She tapped out a quick reply, letting him know she was tired and had ordered pizza. If he pushed, well, she'd call and explain.

His reply was quick and very Danny.

OH. WELL ENJOY. TALK TOMORROW?

Claire nodded and tapped out an affirmative. Tomorrow was a good idea. Maybe by tomorrow she'd have some idea of what words to use and how to say them.

18

Danny parked by the clump of cedar trees in front of Peacock Hill and frowned. Where was Claire's car? She usually left it out front. Surely she wasn't already running errands in preparation for moving to DC? It was barely eight on a Saturday morning. That was early by anyone's standards.

Maybe he should have called first, but he'd wanted to see her. After Tuesday—and the awkward, stilted text conversations they'd had since—he wasn't sure where they stood.

That wasn't entirely true.

He was ninety-nine percent positive she'd dumped him.

But that one percent . . . well, he needed to know for sure.

Danny grabbed the box of doughnuts he'd picked up at the diner in town and started up the steps to the front door. The wreaths on the windows, garlands, and trees definitely screamed Christmas. It was pretty. Maybe knowing if he and Claire still had a chance would help him find his Christmas spirit.

Or it would kill it off completely.

He knocked on the door and waited. Someone was usually

up and moving around on the main floor. If no one came, he'd break down and call Claire.

He waited a couple of minutes then knocked again, a little harder. This time he heard voices.

Jeremiah swung the door open. His hair was sticking up and he had on baggy sweats and a long sleeved T-shirt that had seen better days. "Hey, man. What brings you here?"

"I thought I'd see if I could help Claire. I know she's leaving today." He shrugged. He wasn't going to act excited about it, but he was going to support her. She needed to do this for herself. So she should go do it. Especially if her family couldn't talk her out of it. Had they tried? Or had everyone stood back and let her make what had to be a mistake simply because they were too scared to be the one to ask her to stay?

Jeremiah gave him a long, serious look before stepping back. "Go on in the kitchen. We have coffee."

"Coffee's good. I brought doughnuts." Danny lifted the box a little higher and ambled toward the kitchen, Jeremiah on his heels.

The scent of fresh coffee permeated the kitchen. Danny's mouth watered. He set the box of treats on the island and moved to the pot, at home in the space.

"Hi, Danny. This is a surprise." Deidre looked up from her mug of coffee and glanced at Jeremiah.

"He's here to help see Claire off."

"Oh." Deidre frowned. "That's . . . you . . . when did you last talk to her?"

"Talk?" Danny splashed cream in his mug and carried it to the table. "Tuesday night. It didn't end super well. We've texted a few times, but it's been tense. Awkward. That's why I figured I should just come today. Show her I really do support her in this, if it's what she needs to do."

"Do you? Support her moving?" Jeremiah flipped open the

box on the island and grabbed two doughnuts, dumping them on a paper towel before taking the chair next to Dee.

Danny blew across the top of his coffee and took a long sip. He had to be honest somewhere. With his oldest friend was probably the right place. Even if said friend's wife was the sister of the subject at hand. "I guess. I don't really see that I have a choice. I want her to stay. I want her to be as invested in us as I am. At the same time, I love her enough that if she needs to do this, then I'll do whatever I can to make things between us work. Unless she's already given up. I'm not convinced she didn't dump me on Tuesday. It's one of the reasons I didn't call first."

Deidre closed her eyes and dropped her head on Jeremiah's shoulder.

Jeremiah reached over and covered Dee's hands with his. "Did you ask her to stay?"

"I couldn't. We don't have any legal tie yet. I don't want her to feel like she's rearranging her life because I asked her to. Wouldn't she just wonder forever after that?" Danny shook his head. He'd prayed around and around about it. He was no closer to the right answer. If there was one. "Was I supposed to fight? To beg? But then what if I did change her mind? I don't want her to stay for me. She'd resent me—resent us."

"It wouldn't have mattered." Deidre sighed and tore a piece off one of Jeremiah's doughnuts. "I asked her to stay. I tried to guilt her into it. Whatever I could, I threw it at her. She still left."

Danny started to nod, then cocked his head to the side. "Wait. Left? I missed her?"

"Yesterday. She left yesterday morning."

"Why wouldn't she tell me?" Danny stared into the depths of his mug. They had to be completely over if she could leave without saying goodbye. "We texted last night and she made it sound like she was tucked in here, having pizza. But she was in DC. I guess that answers my question."

"Danny." Deidre reached out to grab his hand.

Danny jerked away. "Don't, okay? I knew it. I knew on Tuesday. And it's okay. It is. I still don't think fighting for her to stay would've been the right thing. And like you said, it might not have mattered. I guess Jamie won after all."

"Jamie? Jamie Fisher?" Jeremiah bit off half of a doughnut, chewed and swallowed. "What's he got to do with any of this?"

"Nothing. Or everything. I guess it depends. Her job is with him. He's been after her personally and professionally since the Founder's Ball at the start of November. He all but outright said she was only dating me because she'd been wanting to for so long she needed to get it out of her system before she could move on with him." Danny hadn't thought his heart could crack open any wider, but it felt as if a huge piece shattered off as he said the words. "He said I was only interested in her because she'd moved on with him. Maybe he was right about that, too."

Deidre murmured something to Jeremiah, slipped off her chair, and waddled from the kitchen.

"You don't believe that." Jeremiah frowned across the table. "Tell me my oldest friend is smart enough not to buy that."

Danny shrugged. At some point, he had to face facts, didn't he? "She's not here. She's in DC with him. Seems pretty clear."

"And you? You only asked her out because of Jamie's interest?"

Danny winced. "It's closer to the truth than I like to admit. She was always there, you know? One of my best friends. Comfortable. Available. And lately, prickly. Honestly, I'm not sure I would have moved in if it hadn't been for Jamie."

"Because you realized . . .?"

"That I loved her. That I wanted—needed—her to be more than my best friend. But it's all too little, too late. She moved on. Literally." Danny tipped his coffee mug making little waves in the surface. What was he supposed to do now?

"And you just let her go?"

"Flip the situation, man. If Deidre had decided to sell Peacock Hill after she finished renovations and move back to DC because she realized the company she had up there was really where God wanted her to be—was where *she* wanted to be— would you have tried to get her to stay?"

Jeremiah pressed his lips together and stared at the wall. He sighed. "I guess not. I would have wanted to, but I understand what you're saying. Love wants the best for the other person— even if what's best for them doesn't feel like what's best for me."

Danny pointed at Jeremiah. "Exactly."

"What will you do?"

That was the million dollar question. "Just keep on, I guess. Maybe God will help her see that DC isn't where he wants her after all. Or maybe God will make it clear to me that she's not the woman He has for me, even though I can't wrap my head around that idea right now. I don't know. I'll keep praying. It's all I can think to do."

"Prayer isn't a last resort though. It's a first line weapon."

Danny closed his eyes. Jeremiah was right. It was easy to forget that prayer wasn't just for when he'd exhausted every-thing he could think to do. It was supposed to be the first thing he turned to. The best thing. Even though his desire to fix it himself made prayer seem like apathy. "Yeah. That's easy to forget."

"For everyone. I'm not great at it either. But I'll pray with you. I know Dee is. Pretty sure Duncan and Anna are, too. None of them were very happy that Claire made the decision and ran off without any conversation or consultation with the family. It's not that she's not an adult and able to do what she wants, but family is important. And it's never a bad idea to seek wise counsel when you're on the verge of completely upending your life."

Danny snorted. "Like when I was going to move to Charlottesville and live with Casey and you helped me think that through?"

"Yeah. Like that." Jeremiah glanced over at the bakery box. "You should eat a doughnut. I'm also pretty sure fat and sugar help with decision making."

This time Danny's snort turned into a full blown laugh. "Yeah, all right. And then, since I came here to work, what can I do to help? If I remember right, you have a group coming tonight for s'mores at the fire pit. There's got to be something that needs doing?"

"You know what? I bet we can find something. Eat that. Drink more coffee. I'll go get better clothes on, and we'll see what we see." Jeremiah carried his mug to the sink and rinsed it out, tipping it into the drying rack.

Danny watched his friend leave and sighed. As much as he wanted to say he could follow Claire to DC if that was what she needed him to do, he wasn't sure he could. Matt and Jeremiah were here. The church he'd grown up in—even if getting away from Mrs. Patterson was a positive—no, he couldn't easily walk away from all of that.

So he'd pray God would bring Claire back home to him.

Soon.

DANNY POWERED up his work laptop and settled back against the sofa cushions. The next episode of his show was on, but he wasn't paying much attention. The longer the season continued, the less he cared. They'd had so many opportunities to resolve the major conflict between the two main characters and not taken them, it was starting to feel like they prolonged it simply for the sake of ramping up the drama. Where it had been an interesting FBI hunts the bad guy kind of show, it was rapidly devolving into a soap opera. Those had never held his interest.

He'd see the season through—there were only four more episodes—and then look for something else.

He opened his email and blew out a breath. His boss had been working this weekend. He scrolled down to the oldest message and clicked it.

His phone rang.

Claire's face lit up his screen.

His stomach sank even as hope constricted his breath. He swiped up to answer.

"Hey, Claire."

"Danny. Hi. I, um, I'm sorry I haven't called you. Deidre mentioned you stopped by yesterday."

"I did. How's DC?"

"I can explain."

"Just don't, okay? On Tuesday I wasn't completely sure you'd dumped me, but I figured it out yesterday. And I get it. I'm old news." He fought to keep his throat from closing. At least his voice sounded steady. Matter of fact.

"No. Danny, no. I didn't—that's not what I want." Claire's voice wavered. "I thought you understood."

"I do. You need to do this for you, to prove something to yourself. And maybe—maybe even if it's not what you think you want right now, maybe it's better. Because you're up there with another guy who interests you and who's interested in you. And maybe you need to explore that and see how it goes. For all the same reasons you needed to take this job and sneak out of town without saying goodbye." He bit his lip. He shouldn't have said the last sentence.

He meant it.

He felt it.

But he still shouldn't have said it.

"I'm sorry. I just couldn't figure out how to tell you."

Seriously? All she had to do was pick up the phone or, even better, swing by and say "Hey, I think I'm going to head out on Friday. I'll be in touch." How was that hard?

"Are you still there?"

"Yeah. I'm not sure what you want me to say."

"Say you forgive me?"

"I do, Claire. I even still love you, but you shouldn't take that into consideration. I'm serious—live your life. Figure things out for yourself. And if you decide you want me in it, you know how to get in touch."

"Danny—"

"Mrs. Patterson told me to tell you hello this morning at church. You might let someone know—Deidre, maybe—that they should spread the word. Matt's aunt thought you were under the weather. I didn't think it was my place to explain." He also hadn't wanted to deal with the inevitable Spanish Inquisition that would follow Mrs. Patterson getting a hold of that information. Let someone else deal with it. Someone whose broken heart wouldn't also be under cross examination.

"Okay. I will. Danny—"

"I should go. I hope you have a really great first day tomorrow, Claire. I'll be praying for you. Thanks for calling. Bye." He ended the call. Maybe it was the coward's way, but he wasn't ready to listen to her explanations and protestations. She said they hadn't broken up. But how long, really, was that reasonable? Especially when she wasn't able to even talk to him and tell him she was leaving town? She'd waited until she'd known he found out from someone else.

That said something about their relationship.

He just wasn't sure what.

19

Claire looked at her phone before dropping it onto the bedspread beside her. Hot tears dripped down her cheek. That probably could have gone worse, but she wasn't sure how. Had they broken up? It sounded like it. She didn't want that.

She didn't want to date Jamie.

Oh, sure, he was rich. And fine, good looking, and nice. But he was also about ten years older than her. In the overall scheme of life, that wasn't a problem if they were meant to be together, but they just weren't. The few dates they'd gone on had made that clear.

And not just because she wanted to be with Danny.

If Danny wasn't an option—*please, Jesus, don't let that be the case*—she still wouldn't choose Jamie.

Now she just had to get both of them to realize that.

Claire wiped her cheek and reached for her phone.

"Hey."

"Hi, Dee. It's me."

"I saw that. What's up?"

"Are you busy? I can call another time." *Please don't be busy.*

Claire leaned back against the headboard and closed her eyes. If she was at home, she would have walked over to Dee and Jeremiah's apartment. She could have hung out with them, or tried to entice Dee to her place with the promise of ice cream.

She'd gotten used to being able to spend time with her sister whenever she wanted. Other than the months Deidre had been down at Peacock Hill before Claire had managed to tie up all the loose ends in DC and get down there, the two of them had never lived far apart.

"No, it's fine. Hang on." There was murmuring in the background before the noise of the TV shut off. "There. Jeremiah went to play a game on the computer. I would have left, but hefting myself out of the couch is too much effort for this late in the day. And my ankles are swollen."

"That doesn't sound good. Are you okay? You still have like six weeks, right?" Had leaving put even more stress on Dee and caused problems with her pregnancy? That would be the icing on the cake.

"I think it's fine. And it's maybe closer to seven? February first. I'm too tired to count it up right now. I should know it, I know. People at church keep asking me and I guess I'm weird that I don't have it all memorized. I know she's measuring thirty-six weeks, and that's bigger than she should be."

"She?" Claire grinned. Deidre had been so secretive about the baby's gender. She and Jeremiah had found out, but they'd decided not to tell anyone.

"Oh, man." Dee huffed out a breath. "Yes. She. But if you tell anyone—especially either of our parents—your life won't be worth living."

"My lips are sealed. It's not like I'm talking to Mom and Dad right now anyway. I don't suppose, since I know her gender, that you want to let her name slip, too?"

"Ha. No. I couldn't if I wanted to. We're still arguing about that. What?" There were scratching and muffled noises then Deidre was back. "Sorry. Jeremiah is correcting me. Apparently we're not arguing, we're discussing."

Claire snickered. A little pang of homesickness settled in her chest. "Okay. Well if you reach the end of your negotiations and have a final decision and you want to accidentally let it slip in my direction, I'd love to know."

"Got it. So. What's up? I don't think you called in hopes of finding out that you were going to have a niece."

"I miss you." Claire pressed her lips together. She hadn't meant to say that. It was true, but what was the point of saying it? This was her choice. No one had made her move. No one had even encouraged it. "That's not why I called though. I talked to Danny."

"Ah. Well, good."

"Is it?"

"Of course it is. You can't have a relationship without communication. You know this, Claire. Even if you didn't know it before Mom and Dad had their psychotic break from reality, surely watching their life implode made it clear to you."

"You have a way with words."

"Yeah, well, I'm still angry with them. And praying that Mom gets some sense knocked into her. Preferably by a speeding car."

"You don't mean that."

Deidre sighed. "You're probably right. But my point is still good. Communication. You can't have a relationship—any kind of relationship—if there's no communication. So you talked to Danny. And?"

"And I think he broke up with me." The last word dissolved into a sob and the tears that had stopped restarted.

"Oh, Claire."

"I know. It's all my fault. And I don't know what to do."

There was a long pause. Claire pulled her phone away from

her ear to check they were still connected. Finally, her sister sighed again. "I can't tell you. That's something you have to figure out for yourself. Even though it pains me. It's the same reason Danny didn't beg you to stay."

"How do you know that?"

"He came by yesterday looking for you. He and Jeremiah had a long conversation—most of the day, to be honest. I got the high points that evening. Which maybe breaks the bro code, but it's absolutely part of the marriage code, so if Danny gets wind and is ticked, he'll have to get over it."

Claire smiled. She could picture her sister explaining in just as many words to an irritated Danny. "I wish he had."

"You wish who had what?"

"Danny had asked me to stay. I wish he had. I . . . I probably would have. Then we wouldn't be in this mess."

"Mmhmm. Now. Now you wouldn't be in the mess. But be honest with me, Claire. Would it have come back to bite him in the tail later? When things got hard and you started looking at that bright green grass on the side of the fence where you don't live, who would you blame?"

Right. Which was why she was in DC in the first place. "You asked me to stay."

"And I shouldn't have. I'm glad it didn't sway you. You have to figure this out for yourself, Claire. No one can do it for you. Danny loves you enough to see that. Now that I'm over my surprise—and I'm getting over my hurt—I can see it too."

"I wasn't trying to hurt you. I wasn't trying to hurt anyone."

"I know that. I think we all do. But you can hurt people without meaning to. It's part of life."

Claire swallowed, but it didn't budge the lump in her throat. "What do I do about Danny? I don't want to lose him."

"Then you need to fight for him."

"He didn't fight for me."

"It's not the same. He wouldn't have been fighting for what he knew you wanted. He would have been trying to convince you to want what he did, at the expense of your dream. But you know he loves you. You know he wants to be with you. So fighting for him? That's just showing him that you want the same thing he does."

"But I told him—"

"Show him. Words are easy. You know that."

Easy sounded about right though. Claire wasn't sure she was up for hard. Besides, what did it even mean to show him? She was starting a new job tomorrow. In DC. She'd given her word, made plans. There were people counting on her here now, too. "I guess."

"You need to pray about it. Then stop talking to God and listen to see what He's saying. You and me and Duncan, we were raised that God gave us good brains, so we needed to handle things and do things based on the use of those brains. But I'm slowly learning, that's not really the point at all. Yes, obviously, we should use our head and not be dumb. But Claire? Having a good brain and strong abilities doesn't mean we have to do everything by our own power. In fact, I think a lot of the time, God's just waiting for us to be willing to say 'you know what, I could probably figure something out here, but I'm going to step back and let You show me what to do.'"

Claire closed her eyes. That first part was absolutely true. How often did she actually rely on God? Only when she'd exhausted everything she could think of—sometimes not even then. "When did you get so wise?"

Deidre laughed. "Blame Jeremiah for that little bit of insight. I'm still a work in progress. We all are. Bonus? Danny understands that, too."

"I love you, Dee."

"Love you too. You okay?"

"No. But I'm hopeful that maybe I will be. Thanks." Claire ended the call and blew out a breath. Had she actually prayed about this job, this move? Oh, sure, she'd done the standard "if it's Your will" thing and asked for roadblocks if it wasn't. Would she have recognized a roadblock? She hadn't been looking. She had been too focused on what *she* wanted. What *she* thought was best.

"I'm sorry, Jesus. Will you help me? I don't know what's right. Or what to do. I do know I don't want to lose Danny—but maybe even that's wrong? Show me Your will. Please."

CLAIRE SPUN her office chair and stared out the window. She could, if she angled just right, see across the river to the Washington Monument. Yesterday had been a typical first day—lots of paperwork and meetings. She hadn't spent more than ten minutes at any one time in her office.

At least she hadn't run into Jamie.

She'd been on edge all day, expecting him to pop in with his gleaming smile and suave words. She absolutely didn't want the people she was working with to think she was only here because the big boss had the hots for her. She didn't even want that last part to be true, but she wasn't sure how to go about making it clear.

Today, so far, had been blissfully quiet. She was working her way through the details about upcoming events and noting where tweaks needed to be made. Who knew a software company would have so many meetings? And sure, they weren't on the scale of a wedding or ball, but they were still important. Taking the honchos of potential customers out—or staying in— to provide a convincing environment that won the business was a new challenge. She could do it. She could do it well.

But it wasn't what she was supposed to be doing. That realization had come at the end of another sleepless night of wrestling with God. Now it seemed so much clearer.

With a sigh, she turned back to her computer and opened a blank email. Turning in two week's notice on the second day of work had to be some kind of record, but it probably wasn't a good one. It was entirely possible they'd just tell her to go, but she was going to lay out a plan of what she could and would do for them over the next two weeks. It would be worth their time and money to let her stay. In fact, it was possible she could get things set up and organized well enough that a current employee could simply take on the work. That would save the company the cost of a full-time employee.

Surely that was worth two weeks of pay?

Claire outlined her thoughts then sat back and re-read the email. It was brief and professional. And it didn't go into the reasons she was leaving. Jamie would suspect, and there was nothing to be done about that, but it wasn't germane to the situation. The truth that had come to her during the past two mostly sleepless nights was that coming to DC was something she'd done completely under her own power and not because it was what God desired for her.

She wanted to be firmly in the middle of His will, not running off doing her own thing and hoping He'd use it for good.

After tweaking a few words and reading through the email one final time, Claire typed in her direct supervisor's name in the "To" field and added Jamie in the "CC." She debated that addition—but the position was designed to work somewhat closely with him. He might as well know right away rather than having to wait for it to wiggle up the chain.

Claire hit send and breathed out.

The weight that had been settled in her chest for weeks loosened and faded away. Now she'd wait.

A glance at the clock in the corner of her monitor showed it was time for lunch. She could slip downstairs and grab a sandwich at the deli on the main floor, maybe find a bench in the little green space between this building and the one next door. With her jacket and the direct sunlight, it shouldn't be too cold to eat outdoors.

Claire locked her computer and grabbed her wallet out of the bottom desk drawer. Snagging her coat off the back of the door, she headed toward the elevators. If she could make it downstairs, she'd be clear until after she ate. And then . . . well, then she'd deal with the aftermath of her course correction.

It was the right thing to do.

It was what she firmly believed God wanted her to do.

Her stomach was still twisted into knots.

20

D anny stopped short, the door to the Greek restaurant banging into the back of his heels and setting off a clatter from the bells tied to the handle. He started to turn. He'd get lunch elsewhere. Or not eat. It wasn't like he'd had a huge appetite since talking to Claire on Sunday night.

"Danny. Don't go." Casey crossed the crowded space and touched his arm. "I've been hoping to run into you."

"Casey. I don't—why?"

"Can we sit? Eat?"

Danny wanted to say no and leave, but his parents had done too good a job training him to be polite. He didn't have a good reason not to, and at some point, he had to eat. "Fine."

She beamed and pointed to the table in the front corner of the space. "I'll be over there."

It wasn't a huge place. He would have seen her. It was probably polite for her to tell him, but he just found it irritating. He gave a curt nod and slid into the short line to order. His previous thought that a gyro was going to hit the spot and untangle the knots of dread in his belly was replaced by the suspicion that this was going to end up being the third day that everything he put in his mouth tasted like dust.

He ordered and paid, carrying the bottle of soda with him to the table.

Casey already had her tray. The food was untouched.

Danny sat and twisted the cap on his bottle. "Well?"

"You don't make things easy, do you?"

He just looked at her.

"Fine. Look. I'm sorry, okay. I didn't figure you'd answer if I called. Or read it if I texted. This was all I could think of. I've been hanging out here for the better part of a week hoping you'd come for lunch. I think the owners are going to be glad to see the back of me."

That teased a smile out of him. The gruff Greek man who ran the restaurant was always as happy as he seemed capable of being to see anyone willing to plunk down their money for some of his food. "I don't know what there is to say. We've been through it all. It hasn't changed."

"I know that. I'm not trying to get you back or anything like that. In fact, I kind of want to start by saying I'm sorry. Except I don't regret the time we spent dating. So maybe it's more like thank you?"

One of the counter workers sidled up and slid a tray of food in front of Danny. He glanced down before nodding his thanks to the man. He closed his eyes and offered a short prayer of thanks for his food then took a fry and dunked it in the tzatziki sauce. "I guess I'm not following."

"You totally just prayed for your food. Right?"

His cheeks warmed and he nodded.

"See, that's what I have to thank you for. For the first time in my life, I saw someone living their faith in little things that went beyond church on Sunday and at Christmas. It made me curious."

He frowned and took another fry. "You never wanted to go with me."

"No. I know. I wasn't curious then. But when we broke up, I started to miss it. There's a contrast between you and the other guys I've dated. I wondered if that might be it. So I went to church."

"Yeah? Good for you."

"It has been, yeah. I'm still not one hundred percent sure about everything, but—"

"Don't do that."

She frowned. "Do what?"

"Don't wait until you're one hundred percent sure. You never will be. I'm still not. I don't think we're meant to be. If we could know for sure on our own, we wouldn't need faith. Take the leap, Casey. Accept Jesus as your Savior. See where it takes you." He scooped up his gyro and took a bite, grateful that the flavors exploded on his tongue instead of disintegrating into the slightly metallic bitterness that had plagued him for three days.

"It's .. are you sure? It's scary."

He nodded. "That doesn't really change either. It gets easier, sometimes. And then it gets harder again. But it's worth it."

Casey chewed her lip, indecision written on her face.

He swallowed and ignored his jumping stomach. "I can walk you through it, if you want."

"Really? You'd do that? After everything . . . why would you do that?"

"Because Jesus is more important than anything else and if there's a chance I can help you embrace that, then I don't want to miss it."

Casey nodded slowly. "The pastor at the church I've been going to says it's easy. Just admitting I'm a sinner and that I need help—that I want the salvation Jesus offers and that He paid for on the cross. Is that really all?"

"That's all it takes to get started, but asking Jesus to be your Savior starts you on a lifelong journey of transformation. God meets us where we are—in all our mucky sin—but He doesn't want us to stay there. He wants to shape us into the image of His Son—Jesus. Which means it's a lifetime of letting go of all the things we think we can do on our own and for ourselves. It's hard and I fail more than I succeed. But like I said, it's a process. A lifetime commitment." Danny looked down at his food and sent up a wordless plea for God to give him the words. He'd never led someone to Christ before. Any talks that got close when he was working with the youth, he tended to shuffle off to Matt or the pastor. Was he even equipped for this?

"That sounds hard."

"Can be. Like I said. But you're not doing it alone. You have the Holy Spirit. You have other believers who help you and encourage you. And in the end, I look back at my life and who I am in Christ, and I wouldn't go back to who I was before that. Even though I was a relatively good person."

"So I just pray? Are there special words I have to say?"

Danny smiled. "No special words. You pray and tell Jesus you're sorry for your sin, that you know you need Him and that you want Him to be the Lord of your life."

"That's it?"

"That's it.

"Right now?"

"Sure." After a moment of hesitation, Danny reached out and took Casey's hand. He closed his eyes and bowed his head.

Casey stumbled through a short prayer. When she paused, Danny offered his own prayer of thanks for Casey and for the gift of salvation.

"I thought I'd feel different."

"You will. You should tell your pastor or someone at the

church you're attending. You'll want to get connected with people who can help you grow and answer your questions."

She nodded. "Can I call you if I have questions?"

That was stickier. He was all for helping new believers, but where was the line with someone who you used to date? "I don't know. I just—things with Claire are weird right now and I don't want to do anything that would make it worse."

"Oh. I'm sorry. Can I help? I mean probably not, but if I can, just tell me how."

Danny shook his head. "I appreciate the thought, but no. I think things just have to run their course. Claire has some stuff to figure out. When she does, I'll be waiting for her to come home."

"You love her."

"I do."

Casey gave a small, sad smile. "She's a lucky girl."

"Thanks. I'm sorry, Casey."

"Don't be. I don't think things between us could have worked. Not where I was. If they did—well, I'm pretty sure I would have ended up hurting you. I really wanted you to move up here. Move in with me. With everything that entailed."

"I know. And I was considering it."

"I'm sorry. I know now—I guess I knew then, too—that would have been really bad for your beliefs. There was a small part of me that wanted you to fall though. I'm not proud of it."

There'd been a part of him—not even a particularly small one—that had wanted it too. Waiting for God's timing—waiting to do things God's way—was hard. At least he was learning. "It's okay. We're good. And I'm glad that out of all of this you found Jesus."

She grinned. "Me too. I'll go and let you eat. Although that's probably soggy now. Do you want me to get you a new one?"

"Nah. It's fine. Take care, Casey. And talk to someone at church. Get plugged in."

Casey stood and gathered her tray. "I will. I'll call the office on my way back to work. Thanks, Danny. For everything. Have a good Christmas—just a week away. You ready?"

Not even remotely. "Nope. I guess I'll get online tonight. I just haven't made the time."

Casey laughed. "I'm not quite finished either. Bye, Danny."

"Bye." Danny watched her leave before turning his attention to his lunch. God really did work everything for good. His relationship with Casey had helped Casey find Jesus. And, in some ways, it had helped Danny be ready to be in a relationship with Claire.

God was good. So Danny would trust that He would bring Claire back home. And if not? Then there was something better in store. He would choose to trust.

~

"You ready for Christmas?" Matt handed Danny a plate and started loading his own with Jeremiah's nachos.

Danny groaned. "Why do people keep asking me that?"

"Because Christmas is on Wednesday. And it's Saturday. So that's like three days away." Jeremiah grinned and carried his plate into the living room. He glanced around before settling on the sofa. "I like how you two have decorated. Much better than when I lived here."

"It's all Azure. I was fine with early bachelor, but she's pretty good at taking thrift store finds and making them feel like home." Matt shrugged.

Danny shook his head. Contentment fairly pumped off both of his friends. Marriage suited them. The familiar pang in his heart barely registered. "I'm not sure about the three days thing. Today is Saturday, so that's one, right? Then Sunday, Monday, Tuesday, and finally Christmas. So five days?"

Jeremiah snorted. "Are you really shopping today? Or Christmas day? That takes out two days. Which leaves three, right?"

"Last time I checked, yes. Five minus two is three." Matt chuckled and carried his own enormous pile of nachos over to the living room. "Please tell me you're finished shopping."

"Basically. I ended up shipping things direct. My folks just decided they were going to go back to my brother's again, even though they were up there for Thanksgiving. I guess his wife couldn't get enough time off to make coming down here enough. And since I can see them whenever . . ." Danny shrugged. It was fine. He understood, and it did make sense. But he was used to having Christmas with his family. "I guess I could look for a flight and go up, too. I get the rest of the week off, so it'd be a decent visit."

"You think there'd be seats still?" Jeremiah dug his phone out of his pocket and tapped at the screen. "Whoa. Good news, there are a handful of seats. Bad news, well, see for yourself."

Danny took his friend's phone and puffed out his cheeks at the prices. "Yeah. No. For those prices I could take a two week vacation overseas. I love my family and, okay, it'll be strange not being around them for Christmas, but that doesn't make sense. I'll be all right."

Jeremiah and Matt exchanged a look.

"You know you're always welcome at Peacock Hill, right?" Jeremiah took his phone back and slid it into his pocket. "I just need to let Dee know more than five minutes before you show up."

"Thanks. I'll think about it." He didn't need to barge in on his friends' Christmas. It wasn't the end of the world to be alone.

"I'll for sure sit with you all at the Christmas Eve service. You're going, right?"

"That's the plan, yeah." Matt glanced at Jeremiah. "Right? Dee's still up for it?"

"Absolutely. The baby makes it hard to sleep—I guess that's a pregnancy thing. She keeps pushing books at me, like I want to read all about late term pregnancy and labor and delivery. I did some Internet searching, and I honestly think I'm better off learning as I go."

"Aren't you going to a class? On TV there's always a class." Matt stood and wandered into the kitchen. "Anyone else want a soda?"

"I do." Danny raised his hand.

"Please." Jeremiah scooped a loaded chip off his plate. "And yes. There's a class. We did that at the start of December. And there's another at the second week of January. Between all of that, I have to believe I'll know what I need to know. Or we'll figure it out."

Danny laughed. "I'm pretty sure you're not supposed to make up parenting out as you go along."

"Don't believe that for a minute, Jer. My aunt—and okay, yes, we should always take what she says with a grain of salt just because of who she is—says that no parenting book will ever prepare you for the real world of having a child. That said, she also sent me a list of books that she thinks we should read. I'll forward it to you." Matt set the sodas on the coffee table and gestured to them.

Jeremiah laughed. "I'm pretty sure she already sent it to us. Dee was trying to decide if she should be grateful or offended."

"Grateful." Matt opened his drink and took a long swallow. "If she wanted you to be offended, you'd know."

Danny grinned. With Mrs. Patterson this was absolutely true. He'd been studiously avoiding her since Claire moved to

DC, but that didn't stop the sad and semi-disapproving looks she cast across the sanctuary at him.

"Now." Jeremiah leaned forward and set down his plate before bracing his hands on his knees and looking at Danny. "The real reason for this little gathering."

Danny's stomach sank. "What do you mean? You said the girls were all going shopping. We haven't had a hang out night in a while. This better not be an intervention."

Matt laughed. "I wouldn't go that far. I mean really, do you see a licensed therapist?"

Danny closed his eyes. "All right. Hit me."

"Claire." Jeremiah crossed his arms. "What are you going to do about Claire?"

Danny sighed. "I love her. You know that. So I did what I had to do and let her go. What am I doing beyond that? Praying that God brings her home."

21

Claire pressed a hand to her stomach to quiet the butterflies. She shouldn't be nervous. Why was she? This was her home. It had been home long enough that there was no need to fear.

Except.

She blew out a breath and pushed open the car door. No one knew she was planning to come for the Christmas Eve service. She hadn't been sure when she'd be able to leave—Jamie had pushed—hard—for her not to quit. Then, when that didn't work, he'd decided her last day couldn't be until today. She could have pushed back, but what was the point? She didn't bear him any ill will—and there had been a few loose ends to finish tying.

She'd loaded the car last night so she could check out of the hotel on her way to the office. There'd been a few bizarre looks in the parking garage, but that didn't matter either.

And now she was back home, hoping her sister had been serious when she'd said there would always be a job for Claire at Peacock Hill.

Hoping—praying—Danny would be willing to forgive.

Tugging her coat collar closer, she trudged across the frozen parking lot. There was no snow in the forecast, but it was cold. A blast of wind buffeted her as she reached the steps to the church.

The soft glow of candlelight and voices singing *Angels We Have Heard on High* greeted her as she crossed the foyer. She'd missed the first fifteen minutes of the service, but at least they were still singing. She hadn't missed the message.

Claire paused at the back of the sanctuary as tears pricked her eyes. Why had she thought she needed to leave this? This was her home. Her family.

She crept along the side aisle until she reached the row where her friends and family stood.

Deidre's eyes grew large when she spotted her and a grin split her face. She squeezed into the aisle and pulled Claire into a tight hug. "You made it! I figured you'd just come in the morning, when traffic wasn't so bad."

"I thought about it. But then I asked myself why. This is where I wanted to be." Claire squeezed her sister back and looked down the row. "Is there room for me?"

"Of course there is. Go on, everyone can bump down one. I want you by me." Deidre clung to Claire's hand.

Claire spied Danny at the far end of the aisle and briefly wished she'd had the self-confidence to strut down the center and slide in next to him. He frowned when Duncan stuck his elbow in his ribs and nudged him over a seat. Then he glanced down toward the end and his gaze locked with hers.

Had he felt the jolt, too?

She lifted a finger and offered a small smile.

Danny winked.

Her throat went dry. Please let that mean what it seemed like it meant. She slid over into the seat beside Jeremiah and smiled at him.

"Stealing my wife, I see."

"Sorry. She was pretty insistent." Claire held up their still joined hands.

Jeremiah chuckled as the music shifted to Chris Tomlin's version of *Joy to the World*. "It's good to see you."

"Thanks." Claire grinned at him then turned her attention to the screens displaying the words and started to sing. Unspeakable joy. That was absolutely what was welling up in her soul. Not just because she was celebrating the birth of her Savior, but because she could see, with absolute clarity, that this was where God wanted her.

The service continued with more songs, readings from Luke chapter two, and a short message on the importance of keeping the why of Jesus' birth in mind. And not just in December, but every day. Claire had a hard time concentrating—her gaze sliding over to Danny periodically to drink in the details of his features.

He only caught her twice.

Well, maybe three times.

Maybe that meant he was struggling just as much as she was.

Finally, the pastor prayed the benediction and the few overhead lights that had been on were turned off and slowly, one by one, the individual candles at each seat were lit as neighbors held their wicks to the flame of the person beside them. In the gentle glow, the pianist began to sing *Silent Night* a cappella and everyone joined in.

When the final strains of the song died out, everyone filed silently from the sanctuary. Claire blew out her candle and dropped it in the bucket that Mrs. Patterson was holding. The woman smiled and opened her mouth as if to speak, but the line of people leaving pushed Claire past her.

Claire let out a relieved breath and shrugged into her coat on the front steps of the church. Arms came around her from behind.

"Hi."

She turned, her face inches from Danny's, and her heart skittered in her chest. "Hi."

"You came home for Christmas."

She nodded. She'd tried for a week to figure out a way to let him know. After a while, she had decided it was better to just show up. "Surprise."

"Best surprise ever. I'm glad I didn't blow my savings on a ticket to Chicago after all."

That would have been a disaster. "Me too."

Danny stepped back and tucked his hands in his pockets. "How long are you here?"

"That's something I'd like to talk to you about. You're coming up to the house, right? For hot chocolate and fireplace s'mores?"

"That's the plan." He searched her face. "Everything okay?"

She nodded. At least she hoped it was. Or it was going to be. "Just . . . things to say."

"I'll see you up there. I'm glad you made it home, Claire." With a nod of his head, Danny melted into the dispersing crowd.

That hadn't gone as well as she'd hoped. Although it had certainly started out well. She could still feel the warmth of his arms around her and that breathless moment when she'd thought he might kiss her.

Of course he didn't. He wouldn't. In his mind, they weren't still together. He was being friendly.

Please, Jesus, don't let him only see her as a friend.

Claire drove up to Peacock Hill, taking in the quiet and darkness of the mountainside. There was no dark, no quiet, in DC. Not like this.

She parked in the shadow of the cedar trees and debated about her car. She could wait and unload tomorrow. Or the day after. Everything she needed for overnight was in her backpack and the box she'd loaded up with gifts. Hefting both, she started up the steps to the front door.

Home.

She was coming home.

Inside she was barely able to set down the box and her bag before being pulled into hugs by everyone, one after the other.

Claire laughed. "You'd think I've been gone a year, rather than a handful of weeks."

"Yes, well, you were missed." Deidre rubbed her arm and pointed to a chair by the fire. "Sit. Everything's nearly ready."

"I can help. I'm not a guest."

Dee shrugged. "Tonight you are."

She didn't want to spoil anything by fighting, so she sat.

Azure settled in beside her. "It's good you're home. We miss you. I hope you'll make it a point to come back as often as you can. I know you'll have your own life in DC, but don't forget we love you."

"I won't." Claire glanced over and studied Azure. She looked paler than usual. "How are you? And the baby?"

"Okay. I have hyperemesis, so basically I get the joy of constant nausea. Most days I throw up four or five times. I'm trying a few things and they're helping some, but I'll tell you what, people who love being pregnant will never be my tribe." Azure swallowed. "Speaking of—you'll excuse me?"

Claire watched as Azure rose and hurried from the room. Yikes. In some ways, though, it was good that she'd had to go. The news that Claire was back for good burned the tip of her tongue. But she wanted to wait until everyone was settled and together, rather than letting it dribble out from one person to the next.

Before much longer, plates of s'more fixings were spread on

the long dining room table and mugs of hot chocolate had been passed around.

Claire sat in the half-circle of her family, a long stick with a marshmallow on the end hovering over the flames in the fire-place, and cleared her throat. "I have some news."

The babble of conversation faded and all eyes turned to her.

Claire pulled her flaming marshmallow from the fire and blew on it to extinguish the flames. Using a graham cracker, she slid it off the stick onto the other half of the s'more on waiting on a plate on her lap. "I'm not just home for Christmas. I'm back to stay. If you still want me."

"Really?" Deidre reached over and clamped her hand around Claire's arm. "You're not playing a prank?"

"No pranks. They don't need me up there. And even if they needed someone, it's not where I need to be. This is home. I want to be home. With my family." Her throat constricted and she took a bite of s'more to cover the emotion.

"That's great, Claire." Jeremiah grinned at her as he poked two marshmallows onto his stick. "I know you said there wasn't that much for you to do here, but trying to cover all that you did is running us ragged. We need you."

Claire smiled but her gaze was drawn to Danny, who sat quiet and still on the other side of the group. What was he thinking? Was he unhappy? She bit her lip. Should she have told him separately?

Danny stood abruptly and strode from the room.

Claire frowned down at her s'more.

"Go after him, Claire." Deidre reached for Claire's plate. "You two need to talk. I know he's part of why you're back. But I'm not sure he knows that."

Claire nodded and stood. She paused at the box of Christmas gifts she'd dropped in the foyer and pulled out a small box. After peeking in the other rooms on the main floor, she peered out the back door. Danny's silhouette was visible climbing the stairs to the gardens.

She pushed open the back door and hurried down the steps of the portico, across the back driveway, and up the stairs.

"Danny! Wait up."

He paused and turned, his shoulders hunched.

"You want to walk down by the pond?" Maybe the extra walk would give her time to sort through the words she needed to say and get them into an order that made sense.

He shrugged.

"Should I not have come back?" Claire fell into step beside him and glanced at his face, trying to make out his features in the moonlight.

"I'm glad you're back. For a visit or to stay, it's good to see you. I've missed you. But. . ."

"But?"

"I guess I don't understand. You had things you needed to prove to yourself. It seems fast."

That made sense. She sighed. "Have you ever gotten somewhere and it just hit you that this place was not where you were supposed to be? You just realize that wow, I made an enormous mistake?"

"Yeah. Once or twice."

"Well, that's what happened. I was already second guessing when I left. It's why I took off without telling you. I was scared that if you asked me to stay I wouldn't be able to say no. It took everything I had to tell Deidre no and to follow through. I thought I needed to do it. I'd convinced myself of that. But when I got up there?" She shook her head. "It all just came crashing down. I realized every piece of me being there was just me. Not God. I hadn't asked Him, not really, what He wanted. So I started doing just that. And He made it so clear. I didn't see the point in prolonging the problem."

They reached the edge of the pond and stopped under the bare branches of a weeping cherry.

Danny reached up and tucked a stray hair behind Claire's ear. "Then I'm glad. I want you to be here for the right reasons. Even if I'm not part of those reasons."

"But you are." Claire reached up and grabbed his hand. "That's part of it. While I was praying—and actually listening for answers—I realized that you're one of the biggest blessings God has ever put in my life. And I'd be stupid to walk away from that. I'm not stupid."

His lips curved. "No. I'd never call you that."

"I love you, Danny. I want to be here, not just because this job with my family is everything I need and want, but also because you're here. And if, down the road, you needed to be somewhere else for your job? I'd want to be there with you. Because I want you to be my family."

"What are you—"

Claire dug the box out of her coat pocket. "Before I left for DC, you asked me if I liked diamonds. I never answered you. The truth is I didn't really know the answer. One of the nice things about DC though? There are a lot of great jewelry stores. So I took lunch breaks and browsed and I realized that yes, I do like diamonds. But I like them best when they're surrounded by something with a little more color. Like an amethyst. So I got this to give to you."

Danny looked down at the box then back at her, confusion evident on his face.

"I love you. I want to spend my life with you. I know you were thinking about marriage before all of this . . . and I really hope you're still leaning that direction." Claire sank to her knee, still holding his hand. "Danny Kent, will you marry me?"

"I think that's my line." He tugged her hand until she stood.

Gingerly, he took the box from her and opened it. He laughed and took out the delicate engagement ring. "This isn't for me."

"Well. It's for you to give to me." He hadn't answered. Maybe she was going about this all wrong, but really, did it matter who asked who? "If you want to?"

Danny pulled her left hand toward him and slid the ring onto her finger. "Yes, Claire McIntyre, I'll marry you. And be your family. If you'll marry me and be mine?"

"You know I will." Claire stepped into his arms as his mouth lowered to hers and they sealed their future with a kiss.

A NOTE from Elizabeth

Don't you just love the happy sigh of a couple *finally* getting their happy ending? Claire and Danny were meant to be together—that was obvious from their very first interaction.

It just took them a while to realize it.

If you missed any of the previous books in the *Peacock Hill Romance* series, why not head back to the beginning and read them from the start? A Heart Restored tells how and why Deidre ended up at Peacock Hill in the first place and is a funny, faith-filled romance.

If you have read all of the Peacock Hill Romance novels and enjoyed them, you can find more stories with relatable characters, realistic problems, and romantic ever afters in any of my other books. Why not start a new series today?

WANT A FREE BOOK?

If you enjoyed this book and want to be the first to know all the news about upcoming books and sales, I'd love for you to join my newsletter. As a thank you gift for subscribing, you'll receive a free download of one of my titles.

Sign up here!

ALSO BY ELIZABETH MADDREY

A Pinch of Promise

A Dash of Daring

A Handful of Hope

A Tidbit of Trust

The 'Grant Us Grace' Series

Wisdom to Know

Courage to Change

Serenity to Accept

Joint Venture

Pathway to Peace

The 'Remnants' Series:

Faith Departed

Hope Deferred

Love Defined

Stand alone novellas

Kinsale Kisses: An Irish Romance

Luna Rosa (part of A Tuscan Legacy)

Non-Fiction

A Walk in the Valley: Christian encouragement for your journey through infertility

For the most recent listing of all my books, please visit my website.

ACKNOWLEDGMENTS

There are always so many people to thank when I hit the end of a book that I'm never quite sure where to begin. Thanks, first and foremost to Jesus, who continues to whisper story ideas in my head and give me the words when I sit down to type. Inevitably, the spiritual lessons my characters learn are part of my ongoing journey of transformation into His likeness as well.

Thanks also to my amazing husband and our boys. They give me space to write and they also know just when Mom's had enough of sitting at the keyboard and is in need of dancing in the kitchen, hiking in the forest, or fixing a snack. I wouldn't want to do life without them.

I'm also greatly indebted to Valerie Comer. She is my cheerleader, a shoulder to bang my head on, and my drill seargent cracking a whip over my head when I need it. She's also an amazing beta reader and, more than anything else: friend. I'm blessed to know you, Val.

I'm also incredibly grateful to Lynnette Bonner and Heather Gray for their conversation, help, and friendship.

Finally, to each of you who have made it to the end of the

book after plunking down your hard earned money for it - thank you. Thank you for reading. For reviewing. For being willing to spend your time in the world that I created. And for coming back for more. You are what makes this all worthwhile.

ABOUT THE AUTHOR

Elizabeth Maddrey is a semi-reformed computer geek and homeschooling mother of two who lives in the suburbs of Washington D.C. When she isn't writing, Elizabeth is a voracious consumer of books. She loves to write about Christians who struggle through their lives, dealing with sin and receiving God's grace on their way to their own romantic happily ever after.

www.ingramcontent.com/pod-product-compliance
Lightning Source LLC
Chambersburg PA
CBHW020411210626
46816CB00006BB/2222